"I need a wife," Reuben murmured. "My son needs a mother."

Ellie tensed. She picked Ethan up and gave him to his father. "You want to fall in love and marry again?"

"*Nay*, I'll marry, but I won't fall in love."

"You'd wed without love?"

"I'd wed for Ethan." He combed his fingers through Ethan's baby-fine hair. "But love? *Nay.* I don't want or need it."

What woman would agree to such an arrangement? "I see." She reached for her satchel on the other end of the counter. "I should get home."

She felt Reuben watching her as she picked up her bag. She was conscious of him as he followed her out of the house.

With a last look in his direction as she pulled away, Ellie wondered how a man who obviously loved his son could dismiss love in marriage so easily. What woman would be happy to be married to such a man and not fall in love with him? And with his son?

Rebecca Kertz was first introduced to the Amish when her husband took a job with an Amish construction crew. She enjoyed watching the Amish foreman's children at play and swapping recipes with his wife. Rebecca resides in Delaware with her husband and dog. She has a strong faith in God and feels blessed to have family nearby. Besides writing, she enjoys reading, doing crafts and visiting Lancaster County.

Books by Rebecca Kertz

Love Inspired

Women of Lancaster County

A Secret Amish Love
Her Amish Christmas Sweetheart
Her Forgiving Amish Heart
Her Amish Christmas Gift
His Suitable Amish Wife

Lancaster County Weddings

Noah's Sweetheart
Jedidiah's Bride
A Wife for Jacob
Elijah and the Widow
Loving Isaac

Lancaster Courtships

The Amish Mother

Visit the Author Profile page at Harlequin.com for more titles.

His Suitable
Amish Wife

Rebecca Kertz

H HARLEQUIN® LOVE INSPIRED®
TM

Recycling programs
for this product may
not exist in your area.

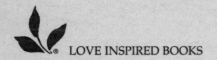 LOVE INSPIRED BOOKS

ISBN-13: 978-1-335-47919-8

His Suitable Amish Wife

www.Harlequin.com

Printed in U.S.A.

Be strong and of a good courage, fear not,
nor be afraid of them: for the Lord thy God,
he it is that doth go with thee;
he will not fail thee, nor forsake thee.
—*Deuteronomy* 31:6

With love for my niece Sarah, my brother's daughter, who has grown up to be a sweet, loving and hardworking young woman. I'm so proud of you.

Chapter One

Elizabeth Stoltzfus stared at the small residence surrounded by a yard filled with junk—wood scraps, rusted cars and other debris she couldn't identify. She'd been cleaning houses for years now, but she'd never seen a place like this. The family who'd recently moved to their church district lived here? This was the place the bishop wanted her to clean?

She frowned. The house wasn't large enough for a typical Amish family, and it certainly wasn't big enough to warrant a cleaning lady. But she'd do it because Bishop John had asked her, although she was afraid of what she might find inside.

She steered her buggy to the end of the driveway, where she secured her horse to the hitching post, which looked brand-new. Ellie reached into the back of her vehicle for her cleaning supplies, including her broom. When she cleaned houses for the English, she used her clients' vacuum cleaners. Her corn broom or a damp mop was the best way to clean Amish floors, most of which were made of wood or linoleum.

She approached the side door with her plastic supply

tote in one hand and broom in the other. She leaned the broom handle against the building and rapped hard on the door. A child's high-pitched cry rent the silence before the door opened. A young woman with a baby on her hip studied her, then saw the supplies and smiled with relief.

"Sarah Miller?" Ellie realized the woman was actually a teenage girl.

"*Ja*, I'm Sarah. Come in," she said as she moved aside to allow Ellie entry. "You're here to clean for us, *ja*? Thanks be to *Gott*. The house needs it badly."

With a smile, Ellie quietly took in her appearance. Sarah wore no head covering, and tendrils of hair were pulled out as if she or her baby had tugged on the blond locks. Her light blue tab dress was stained with what looked like baby food and who knew what else. She had dark circles of exhaustion under her eyes.

"The bishop sent you."

Ellie nodded. "You're the one who spoke with him, then? He's a *gut* man." She meandered around the room, taking stock of what needed to be done, which looked to be a great deal. "Is there any particular place you want me to start?"

She hid her horror at the condition of the kitchen as she tied on her apron. The floors were stained and warped, and the walls needed several coats of white paint. The countertops didn't look much better. She wondered why this young family had moved here and about the state of their finances.

"You can start here, in the kitchen," the girl said, gesturing about the room. The baby cried louder, and Sarah tried to soothe him.

Ellie felt bad for the young mother, who looked ready

to keel over. The girl clearly needed her rest. She'd offer to hold the little boy, but she had a job to do and the work had to be completed first. She grabbed her broom and started on the floor, which was covered with dust and dirt. With even sweeps of the corn broom bristles across warped wood, she swept the filth into a pile, then onto a metal dustpan, which she dumped outside.

The floor done, she began to wipe down the countertop with a wet, soapy sponge. After checking inside the cabinets, she removed the meager contents and ran a damp sponge over the shelves. Sarah had left the room. She could hear the baby crying from upstairs. Trying to ignore the sound, Ellie did what she could to clean the kitchen. The stove looked new and required little but a damp cloth. She spent a good amount of time on the small gas-powered refrigerator at the end of the counter, removing the food that was inside—a carton of eggs, milk, a pack of sausage and a few other items—and scrubbing it inside and out. It was a heavy task, for it looked as if the appliance hadn't been used in a long time and the last person who'd owned it hadn't taken the time to clean it thoroughly. Satisfied with the results, she went into a back room where she found a gas-powered freezer along with washer and dryer. She checked over each appliance, pleased to find them in better condition.

The baby continued to wail as Sarah descended the stairs, the sound growing louder as she approached. Ellie came out of the back room.

"I'm sorry," the girl apologized. "I can't get him to stop."

"May I hold him?" Ellie asked gently, softening her gaze.

"Ja, danki." Sarah handed her the child.

The baby instantly quieted in her arms. "What's your *soohn*'s name?"

The girl shook her head. "He's not my son. He's my nephew. I've been watching him for my *bruder* while he works." She eyed the baby helplessly. "Ethan," she murmured sadly. "His name is Ethan."

"I see." Gazing into the baby's bright blue eyes, Ellie smiled. "Do you have a clean diaper?"

"*Ja*, but I don't think it will help. I just changed him."

"Has he eaten?"

Sarah glanced at her wristwatch. "'Tis not time."

"Babies know when they are hungry. Do you have milk for him?" The girl nodded. "Will you make up a bottle?" Sarah proceeded to fix it. "Where's his mother? She busy, too?" Ellie asked, curious.

"She's dead. She died right after she gave Ethan life."

"I'm sorry," Ellie said with genuine sympathy, although she believed that the woman was in a better place. God would have taken her into His house and made her happy that she'd sacrificed her life for her son's.

Sarah approached with the bottle and reached for the boy.

"May I feed him?" Ellie watched her closely. "Why don't you wash up," she suggested softly after Sarah nodded. "Do you have fresh garments?"

"*Ja.*"

"Go, then, and take a few moments for yourself. You deserve it. I'll watch Ethan for a while until you feel better."

"*Danki,*" Sarah murmured shyly before she headed upstairs.

Ellie heard the slam of a door. "Sarah?" a man's voice boomed. "How's Ethan?"

He entered the room and froze when he saw her. She released a startled breath as she recognized him. The baby's father was Reuben Miller, her sister Meg's former sweetheart, the one who'd lost control of his buggy one rainy night and sent Meg into the cold, dark depths of a creek.

"Ellie?" he said unhappily. "Ellie Stoltzfus?"

"Reuben," she greeted, acknowledging that she knew him.

"What are you doing here?"

"I'm cleaning house."

He scowled. "Why?"

She raised her chin. "Because the place needs it, and—"

"And?" he prompted.

She stared at him. He was sweaty and disheveled but still an attractive man. He had removed his straw hat and his blond hair was matted. Golden hair a shade darker than the hair on his head ran along his jaw, the beard proclaiming him as having married. But it was his eyes that drew her attention the most. They were a beautiful shade of blue, like the light blue of a bright sunny summer sky. His features were strong and symmetrical. She suffered a fluttering like butterflies in her belly. Reuben Miller was an extremely handsome man.

"Ellie?"

"Bishop John told me to come."

"I didn't ask for someone to clean for me."

He clearly didn't want her here. She saw his face change as he realized that she was holding his child. Reuben approached and extended his arms.

Clutching the baby closer, she resisted his unspoken request and stepped back. "I won't hurt him."

He sighed. "I know you won't." The man closed his eyes, looking tired beyond measure, and Ellie felt a deep welling of sympathy for him.

With a soft murmur for Ethan, she gave Reuben his son, then turned for her cleaning supplies with the intent to continue on to the next room. To her surprise and relief, the baby snuggled against his father's chest without a whimper.

"Ellie?" Reuben said when she headed toward the gathering room beyond the kitchen.

"Ja?" She faced him.

"I don't need you here."

She flushed with anger. "I'm not here for you, Reuben. I'm here for Sarah and Ethan." After a brief pause, she added, "If you have a problem with me, talk with the bishop." Ignoring him, she began sweeping the floors in the other room, hoping he would stay away and not give her grief.

The ensuing silence in the house unsettled her. Reuben hadn't followed to harass her, and his absence after their mild altercation worried her. She returned to the kitchen for a peek, and what she saw made her heart pause before it started to pump harder. Reuben leaned against the counter cradling his son as he fed the baby his bottle. She experienced an odd sensation in her chest as she watched man and child together. Suddenly, Reuben looked up as if sensing her presence. They locked gazes, and she lurched back a few steps, eager to escape the odd intimacy of witnessing a tender moment between a father and his son.

"Ellie!" Sarah bounced down the stairs and stopped

abruptly when she saw her brother. "Reuben, you're home! How was work? Did your crew get the job done? Will you have time to work on the *haus* tomorrow?"

Expecting him to scold his sister, Ellie was shocked to see his face soften with indulgence as he smiled at Sarah. Reuben chuckled, and the sound rippled along her back from her nape to her lower spine. "In answer to your questions—*ja*, I'm home. *Gut*, work was *gut. Ja*, we got the job done. And as to your last question, most definitely *ja*." He'd held up a finger with each yes, the last of which caused Sarah to squeal with pleasure.

"You've met Ellie," Sarah said with a smile.

"We're acquainted," Ellie confessed, meeting the girl's light blue eyes. She transferred her attention to Sarah's brother. "I didn't know you'd married. It must have been soon after…" She bit her lip, her voice trailing off before she could mention his breakup with Meg.

"I met Susanna not long after," he began. "We married six months later." He studied his son. "We were happy until…"

"'Tis *oll recht*, Reuben," his sister said softly. "I know how hard this is for you, but I'm here to help for as long as I'm able."

His smile for Sarah was soft and filled with affection. "I know you wish to be with our family in Ohio. I appreciate that you're here for now. I'll find someone to take care of Ethan so you can go home."

"I don't mind being here, *bruder*."

"I know you don't." Sorrow settled on the man's features, touching something deep inside Ellie. "But you're too young for this worry."

Overwhelmed by conflicting emotions, Ellie turned

away. "I'll finish the gathering room and return tomorrow to do the bedrooms and baths."

"Ellie—"

"Don't say you don't need me to clean for you, Reuben, because from the look of this place, you most certainly do."

She caught a quick glimpse of anguish on his features as he turned away. Her gaze once again moved about the room. Was he concerned with money? She didn't know what to say to make him feel better that wouldn't offend him. She had no intention of being paid for the work. Reuben and his family needed her, and she was always happy to help someone in need. If she told him that, however, she knew he'd glare and order her to leave. Now that she understood the situation, leaving was the last thing she wanted to do.

She returned to the gathering room to dust the furniture. After a brief visit to the kitchen sink to fill up her bucket, she worked to scrub the walls. As the grime fell away, leaving the room brighter, Ellie smiled. It always felt good when she could see the fruits of her labor, and the new look of the room was a vast improvement.

"Ellie." Reuben's quiet voice startled her. She gasped and spun to face him. She looked behind him, but there was no sign of Sarah.

"Is something wrong?" she asked. Ellie saw that he'd noted the bright cleanliness of the room. "Do you need something?"

His lips firmed. "I don't think you should come back tomorrow."

She lifted her chin. "Then don't think, because I will return, Reuben. You have a baby to consider. He should have a clean place to crawl." She narrowed her gaze as she took his measure. "Is it because it's me? You're angry because I'm Meg's sister?"

He looked shocked. "*Nay!* The fact that you and Meg are related has nothing to do with this."

She went soft. "This isn't paid work for me. I'm here as a favor to Bishop John."

"I can pay," he said sharply.

"Reuben—" She started to object, but he'd left the room.

Ellie closed her eyes as she sighed. The man needed help, but clearly accepting it didn't sit well with him. She thought of young, tired Sarah and felt rising sympathy for the teen. She firmed her resolve. She'd be back whether or not Reuben Miller liked it. She'd do all she could to help Sarah and the baby. Short of his throwing her bodily out, she'd return tomorrow and the next day for as long as she could help in any way.

A glance at her wristwatch confirmed that it was late afternoon. She'd started the work at one, after having finished housecleaning for the Smith family, English clients. Tomorrow she'd come after she worked at the Broderick house. She made a mental list of what this house—Reuben—needed as she searched through every room on the first floor. She gathered her cleaning tools, then left after calling out to Sarah that she was leaving.

Ellie was conscious of Reuben's stare on her through the kitchen window as she climbed into her buggy and left.

Reuben held his sleeping son close as he watched Ellie Stoltzfus leave. He'd never expected her to come here, and it bothered him that she had. The house was a disaster, and he was ashamed with how little he'd been able to get done.

He'd known the house and land needed work. His uncle had purchased the property from a poverty-stricken English family who'd needed the money desperately. It had always been Uncle Zeke's intention to clear the land and fix up the house for him and Aunt Mary to live out their remaining years, but then Aunt Mary had passed on, and he'd gone into his own decline. When Zeke died, the house went to his only remaining relative, his brother, who was Reuben's father, who gave it to Reuben after his wife Susanna's death.

When he'd first married Susanna, he'd made plans to build a house for them on a section of his father's farm. They had lived with his parents for the first months while Reuben had saved nearly every dollar he'd earned from his construction job. They'd been excited when he learned Susanna was pregnant. They decided to remain in his parents' house during Susanna's pregnancy and wait until after the baby was born to start construction on their home. But then everything in his life had changed after his wife died within minutes of delivering Ethan. He'd gained himself a son but had lost his life partner, and he'd been devastated. He'd barely been able to think. It had hurt too much to feel, to breathe, yet he was responsible for the tiny newborn he and Susanna had made together.

Susanna's medical bills and funeral had taken all of his savings, and he was left with no choice but to stay with his parents until he could finish paying off his late wife's hospital bill while trying to save whatever money he could to have a place of his own. During those awful first grief-filled months, his mother and sister had stepped in to care for Ethan while he took every opportunity to bury his grief with work. Then Mam and Dat had decided to move to Ohio to be closer to Mam's parents. Dat had suggested that he and Ethan move with them, but Reuben hadn't been able to bear the thought of another change in his life. When his father gave him Uncle Zeke's property, it had been like an answer to Reuben's prayers. After his parents had sold their property, Reuben had moved into Uncle Zeke's place. It was a disaster, but he could fix it up and make it a home. His sister Sarah had offered to stay and help with Ethan until Reuben could make other arrangements for his son's care while he was at work.

Life was tough. He worked hard to feed and clothe Ethan, and although he'd finally paid the balance owed to the hospital, there never seemed to be enough money or time to fix up the house and clear the garbage from the yard. He briefly closed his eyes. *So much to worry about.*

Reuben knew the best solution would be for him to marry again, something he didn't want to do. Still, he had to think of his son first, so he would find a wife, if only for Ethan to have a mother. He would need to find a woman who would watch and protect his son and be content to simply be a quiet, calming companion for him. He wouldn't promise love, although he would honor her. He didn't want to marry for love. Love hurt too much.

He would be practical in his choice of bride. He'd already lost a wife. While Susanna and he had started their relationship as friends, deep affection and love for each other had come with time. When she died, a part of him had died with her. He never again wanted to feel that depth of pain.

"Reuben, are you hungry?" Sarah entered the room with a smile. "I can make us eggs, toast and sausage."

"That sounds *gut*, Sarah." He smiled his thanks while he noted something different about her. She looked rested, pretty. She'd redone her hair, and the dress she wore looked freshly laundered. It was only at that moment that he realized how hard it must be for her to care for his young son. His sister was only fifteen, and she received no help or relief from Ethan's care, except for when Ethan was napping. It wasn't fair for Sarah to be saddled with a child. He would have to start looking for a wife, and soon.

Reuben shifted his son in his arms and softened as he studied Ethan's perfect, smooth baby facial features. His son lay content against him. It had taken him a while to bond with Ethan. His grief had been too stark, at first, that it had been painful to look at his son, who reminded him of Susanna. But his parents' decision to move had spurred him to change and take full responsibility and care of his child. He'd held his baby frequently, staying up with him at nights when he cried. He'd bathed, fed, and changed his diaper. His time spent with Ethan had created a deep parental bond. He'd discovered a love for his son that was overpowering and joyful. Every time he saw the way his baby lay trustingly within his arms, his love overflowed, overtaking his grief and cementing an even stronger link. There wasn't anything he wouldn't do for his child—and that included taking another wife so Ethan could have a mother.

After supper, he left Ethan in Sarah's care and built a cradle large enough for a toddler to use on the first floor for when he and Ethan were downstairs together. Tomorrow, he would work to replace old and damaged shingles on the roof of his house. The job shouldn't take long. The area of roof was small, but the house had two floors, with the bedrooms and bathroom upstairs and a second smaller bath downstairs. Plenty of room for three or four, even possibly five people. *Although there will be only three of us living here.* He had no intention of having more children. He'd learned the hard way that the health risk to a woman was too great.

The next morning, he got up and checked on Ethan, who continued to sleep. He began to assemble what he'd need to fix the roof. He briefly considered bringing Ethan outside while he worked, but was afraid that his son would get hurt as he stripped off shingles and tossed them to the ground. Ethan would have to remain inside with Sarah. Today, he'd get a lot done with the building supplies that he'd already purchased and stored in the small barn. Money was tight, but he would get paid by the construction company in the next couple of days.

Reuben felt a measure of peace at his plans for the day, until he remembered that Ellie Stoltzfus had said she'd be back. His good humor and sense of well-being abruptly left him.

He sighed as he recalled the first time he saw her years ago...sweet, lovely, with golden blond hair and bright blue eyes. He'd been attracted to her.

He forced the memory away. He had to stick to his plan and find a wife who would accept that they would be companions but nothing more. The last thing he needed was for Ellie to interfere with his life. He had enough to worry about without the attraction he still felt complicating things.

Chapter Two

Ellie had no idea why she felt as if she shouldn't tell her family about Reuben. Yet she decided not to tell anyone about her experience at the house or that Reuben had moved into their church district. They'd find out soon enough when Bishop John introduced him to the community, or in the event that someone such as their neighboring busybody, Alta Hershberger, learned about the new family in Happiness and nattered about them.

She told him she'd be back today. And she'd made the decision to return tomorrow and the day after that until he no longer needed her. But once she'd arrived home last evening, she'd worried about the cleaning jobs she already had scheduled. Ellie couldn't abandon her housecleaning business yet, even if she wanted to help someone in need. She'd worked too hard to get it going, and she wasn't about to let any of her clients down now that they'd come to rely on her. Thankfully, the Broderick family, her job for this morning, had changed the day and time that they wanted her to clean. Which left Ellie free to head to the Reuben Miller residence first thing to continue the work she'd started yesterday afternoon.

The early summer day heralded warm temperatures and sunny skies. Ellie enjoyed the trip to Reuben's as she viewed the green lawns that looked lusher after an overnight rain. She was happy with her life and pleased with how well her cleaning business was doing. She figured she would clean houses until she had children after marrying.

She wasn't in any hurry to wed. Her sisters Nell, Leah and Meg were happy with their husbands, and her youngest sister, Charlie, would be marrying Nate Peachy, the man she loved, come autumn after harvest time in November. Once Charlie moved out of the house, Ellie knew that she would be the only one there to help Mam and Dat with chores. Her parents were getting older, and she noticed that they were starting to show their age. She caught her father walking with a stiff gait as if in pain, especially before it rained. Her mother often needed help lifting baking pans out of the oven, and she seemed to have slowed down some. Though she was away from the house with her work each day, Ellie always made it a point to help them in any way she could when she was home.

The house would be too large for her parents if she wed and left the nest like her sisters. If her mother and father were settled in a smaller home, Ellie would feel better about moving on. But as things stood, with five daughters and no sons to take over the property, there would be no one to help her *mam* and *dat* if she left. And there was no *dawdi haus* on the property, since neither Mam nor Dat had parents who lived in the area. Her *dat*'s *eldre* were deceased, and her *mam*'s non-Amish parents lived in Ohio. For now, she'd keep a close eye on them. If they needed her, she could adjust her cleaning schedule to spend more time at home.

Ellie saw Reuben immediately as she steered her horse onto the short driveway next to his house. He knelt on the roof, working on removing shingles. He wore his black-banded straw hat to protect his face and neck from the sun and a short-sleeved light green shirt with black suspenders and navy tri-blend work pants. As she climbed down from her vehicle and tied up her horse, she heard the *thud*, *squeak*, *thud*, *squeak* of his hammer claw as he pried nails out of old roof shingles before he ripped them up and tossed them to the ground.

She stood a moment, her hand shadowing her eyes against the sun so she could see him better. She couldn't help but notice the way his forearms flexed as he worked. Reuben moved to another area to tear off a section of the roof, then suddenly stopped as if he'd sensed her presence. He stared down at her, his expression unreadable. He rose to his feet as if planning to come down, and she feared that the wood might not be sturdy enough to hold his full weight. Sorry to have disturbed him, she turned away without a word, hoping that he wouldn't follow. She didn't want to get into a discussion with him when he was that high off the ground, and she didn't want him to send her away before she could finish cleaning his house.

Heart thudding, she retrieved her cleaning tools and approached the side door of the house. To her surprise, the door opened, and Sarah waited with a smile and warmth in her expression. There was no sign of Ethan.

"You came back!"

"I said I would."

Sarah nodded. "I know you clean houses for a living and that you have other work that needs to get done. I don't expect you to ignore it to help us."

"Not to worry. The family I was going to clean for this morning rescheduled. Even if I have to work, Sarah, I'll clean for you. I may have to come later in the day, but I will come," Ellie said softly. "I always keep my word, and I want to help."

Sarah blinked back tears. *"Danki,"* she whispered. She followed as Ellie set her supply tote on the bench behind their dining table. "I can't believe how good the great room looks after you scrubbed the walls," the girl said. "Reuben wants to paint every room in the house, but there is so much else to do, he had to decide what needed to be done most urgently."

"Like the roof." Ellie sorted through her supplies. "That makes sense. You never know when it will rain. Water damage is hard to fix." She pulled out a foaming spray, a roll of paper towels and window cleaner. "Your *bruder* knows what he is doing."

"I know." The girl sighed. "I wish I could do more for him. He hasn't been the same since Susanna died."

"I'm sorry. It must be hard for him having a son so young."

"'Tis. But at least I can be there for Ethan."

"Ja, but what about your plans?"

"I'm fine. Once Reuben finds someone to care for Ethan, or if he chooses to marry again, then I'll join my *eldre* in Ohio."

Ellie studied her with warmth and compassion. "You haven't been out of school long."

"I finished eighth grade last session."

She smiled. "You're a *gut* sister, Sarah."

The girl shrugged. "He's family. You do what you can for family and friends."

"Wise as well as compassionate," Ellie murmured with a smile. "I'm going to tackle the bathroom." There was no sign of Ethan. She looked around, wondering if someone had taken the baby to help out. "Where's your nephew?"

"Sleeping." Sarah grinned. "Hard to believe given the noise Reuben is making, but he's asleep in the other room. Last night Reuben made him a large cradle for the great room. I was able to feed him, then rock him to sleep."

"Then you'd better enjoy the moment. I'd say peace and quiet, but clearly you don't have that," Ellie said drily as she glanced toward the ceiling.

The teenager laughed. "That I don't."

When she entered the bathroom, she was surprised to see that it was amazingly clean.

Ellie sought out Sarah. "Who cleaned in here?"

"Reuben," the girl said. "My *bruder* likes a clean *haus*, which is why this—" she gestured all around her "—upsets and embarrasses him."

"I can help. He has enough to do." She was actually shocked that the man had done work that most of the men in their Amish community wouldn't touch because they considered it women's work. She must have spoken her thoughts aloud, because Sarah answered her.

"Reuben helped Susanna during her pregnancy. He doesn't mind doing women's work."

"An unusual man," she murmured beneath her breath. Ellie saw that Sarah looked much better today, with bright eyes, clean clothes and hair rolled and pulled back neatly into the style of Amish women. Reuben, she realized with an odd pang in the center of her chest, cared about his sister's well-being and probably made time for chores so Sarah wouldn't be overworked.

She swallowed hard. She didn't want to think well of him. Her sister Meg had mooned over him for a long time after she met him at a youth singing one summer a few years back. Reuben had belonged to another church district and hadn't come back to visit until nearly two years later. Then he'd finally shown an interest in her sister. He'd offered to take Meg home from the singing and she'd agreed. It had been a rainy night as Reuben steered his buggy along a back road as he drove her home. A speeding car had rounded a bend, forcing his buggy off the road, down an incline and into a creek. Reuben and Meg had ended up in the hospital; Meg's injuries were a concussion and a severely fractured leg. Reuben had suffered a worse concussion that had affected his memory of the crash.

Reuben's attention toward Meg before and after the crash had been caring and courteous. But Meg had realized early on that she'd fixated on him because she'd been trying to forget her feelings for Peter Zook. She'd continued to see Reuben, feeling as if she owed him after he'd saved her life, but then she realized that she couldn't allow Reuben to court her when she was in love with Peter. After Peter and Meg discovered they were meant for each other, her sister had realized that it was Peter, not Reuben, who had rescued Meg from the creek. Despite his foggy memory of that night, Reuben had known he couldn't swim and probably hadn't saved her. But when everyone had told him he had, he'd believed it because he'd wanted it to be true.

Once Meg ended her relationship with him, Reuben had no choice but to let her go.

Reuben as he'd looked years ago and the way he appeared now suggested he had suffered in the intervening years. Ellie didn't want to think about Reuben or his suffering. She forced him from her mind as she went upstairs to find the other bathroom as clean as the one on the first floor. She entered a bedroom where she began to dust furniture. Once finished, she picked up a broom, dust cloth and lemon polish, then left the room. And found herself blocked by Reuben.

She gasped. His imposing nearness stole her breath. She eyed him warily as he stood before her with perspiration staining his shirt and beading on his forehead. He smelled like man and hard work, and the scent wasn't unpleasant. "Reuben! You frightened me."

He didn't smile. Instead he narrowed his gaze and stared at her. "I thought I told you that I didn't need you." His lips firmed. "The *haus* is already clean."

"You cleaned the bathrooms."

He nodded. "And the rest of the *haus*."

"I'll just go over the bedrooms again lightly so you won't have to worry about them for a few days."

"Elizabeth," he began, and she jerked at the use of her proper name.

"Reuben, please," she pleaded, wondering why she was trying so hard. "Just let me do the work. It won't take up much time and then I'll be out of your hair and gone." She bit her lip. "And 'tis Ellie."

She was shocked to see a small smile settle upon his masculine lips. "You are surprised I know your given name."

After a brief hesitation, she inclined her head. "My name could have been Ellen or Eleanor."

The good humor reached his eyes, startling blue in intensity, as he studied her. "But it's not. It's Elizabeth."

"How did you know that?" Then it hit her. For whatever reason, Meg must have mentioned it to him.

He shrugged. "Why does it matter?"

She stiffened. "It doesn't."

Reuben masked his expression as he took in the supplies she held. "How long will you be here?"

"No more than an hour."

He assented with a jerk of his head. "Fine. When you're done for the day, consider yourself absolved of doing anything more. You can tell Bishop John that you did your duty."

But what about tomorrow or next week? The man, like his sister, was stretched to the limit. Ellie had the strongest urge to convince him that it would be best if she cleaned his house on a regular basis. There was too much for him to do to worry about the inside of the house. He had his construction job—Meg had told her about it—and his work fixing up the house and a messy yard to clear. He might think she'd agreed because of her silence, but she would come back whether or not he liked it.

Reuben spun on his heels and left. Less than five minutes later, she heard him on the roof again. This time the sound was of him nailing down new shingles; the noise continued for the rest of the time she was there. When she went downstairs before leaving, it was to find Ethan awake and on Sarah's hip. The eight-month-old saw her and gave her a sloppy grin. When he extended a chubby hand toward her, Ellie took it and kissed the back of his fingers.

"All done," Ellie said to Sarah as she gathered up her supplies.

"Will you be back?"

Ellie glanced toward the back door. "I'll try. Your *bruder* doesn't want me here, but I think 'tis best if I return, don't you?"

Sarah bobbed her head. "*Ja*, please. I'll handle Reuben." She gazed at her surroundings. "Can you come back next week?"

"*Ja*, I'll have to check my work schedule, but I can always come after one of my other jobs." Ellie smiled at the girl as Sarah accompanied her to the door.

"Ellie?"

She met the girl's gaze. *"Ja?"*

"Can you teach me how to make a few recipes? I never cooked much while I was growing up. I have older sisters who did most of the cooking. I'd like to make Reuben something more than breakfast or sandwiches for supper. I'm sure he is especially tired of eggs, toast and sausage, although he never complains."

Warming to Sarah, Ellie grinned. "I'll find some simple recipes to start." She lowered her voice to a whisper. "And I'll bring the ingredients so Reuben will be surprised."

The teenager beamed at her. *"Danki*, Ellie."

"You are more than *willkomm*. I'll see you next week unless you're visiting on Sunday. 'Tis Visiting Day."

Sarah shook her head sadly. "Not this week. Reuben isn't ready to go visiting."

"I understand." And Ellie did. The man was going through a lot with having to raise Ethan on his own after losing his wife. She felt overwhelmed by compassion for him. He'd had a tough time, and he still had a long road to travel before he'd feel as if God had blessed him with a good and happy life.

"Any particular dishes Reuben likes?"

"Chicken corn chowder and strawberry pie."

"I'll see what I can do," Ellie promised before leaving.

Reuben had finished the roof. It was almost noon when he climbed down the ladder and headed in to wash up. He rounded the house and saw Ellie. She was loading her cleaning implements into the back of her buggy. She stepped back and untied her apron strings, then folded the garment neatly and placed it on the seat with her supplies. She turned to walk around to the other side of the vehicle and saw him. He saw her stiffen and raise her chin.

Reuben experienced a tightening in his chest. She was beautiful, and it wasn't the first time he'd noticed her. In fact, he'd thought her pretty as a young teenager. The shade of her light blond hair and her bright blue eyes were striking. But she'd been just a kid, younger than Meg, who'd been quick to smile at him and draw his attention. While he may have glanced occasionally Ellie's way, he'd known that she was too young for him. He'd wanted to get married, and Meg was the right age. And she was pretty like her sisters, although her coloring was different.

When he'd asked to take Meg home after the first singing he'd attended in their church district in years, he'd felt comfortable in Meg's presence. He'd liked her a lot. After the next singing, when she'd agreed to ride with him again, he'd felt as if he was on to something. He had easily imagined Meg as his wife…until it had all gone wrong, and he'd been forced to walk away and not look back. Not toward Meg, who he'd discovered was in love with Peter Zook. Not toward Ellie, who had still been too young to be a wife or mother.

Now, he was hungry and thirsty as he entered the house. Sarah turned from the kitchen counter with a sandwich on a plate for him. She smiled as she handed it to him. "'Tis just strawberry jam with peanut butter," she said.

He grinned. "Just what I needed." He looked around the room. "Where is Ethan?"

"Napping again."

"He's able to sleep through all the noise?"

Sarah nodded. "He's a sound sleeper."

Reuben took a glass from the cabinet and filled it with water. Then he sat at the table to eat his sandwich. "Have you eaten?"

"*Ja.* I decided to take advantage of Ethan's nap time."

"Ellie left?" he asked, knowing well that she had.

"*Ja.* She did a *gut* job with the house. Perhaps you should let her wash all the walls."

He tightened his jaw. "I'll buy the paint tomorrow so I can start on the rooms downstairs."

"Why don't you like her?" Sarah studied him curiously.

"I like her well enough. What makes you think I don't?"

"You weren't very pleasant to her. She only came to help."

"I don't need her charity, Sarah."

"She doesn't consider helping us charity, Reuben.

She's a nice woman. She likes helping her friends." Sarah paused. "She's my friend."

Reuben softened his expression. "You're easy to like, Sarah. Everyone can't help but love you."

To his surprise, his sister blushed. "When do you have to go back to work?"

"Monday. Mike has a new job he wants us to start."

"I wish you didn't have to work so hard," she murmured.

"I don't work any harder than you do."

"*Ja*, you do, Reuben. I wish I could do more for you."

"You do more than enough, Sarah. I shouldn't have allowed you to stay. You're a young woman and you have your own life to live."

He heard Ethan whimper from the other room. Sarah went to check on him but was back within seconds. "He settled again," she told him.

Reuben rose and went to the sink, where he washed his dishes. "Why don't you take a walk?" he suggested. "'Tis beautiful outside."

She grinned. "I think I will."

He watched his sister leave the house with sadness. He shouldn't have allowed her to stay behind when his family moved. But he'd had no idea how he would manage without a caretaker for Ethan. He had to fix the house and to work to provide for Ethan and so he had the money for paint and building supplies. He glanced down at the kitchen floor with a frown. It was in terrible shape. When he selected the paint, he'd have to price new wood for the floor.

An image of Ellie settled in his mind. She was a hard worker. She'd gotten the house cleaned in a short time, especially considering how bad everything was.

He'd tried his best to do what he could, but his work schedule mostly kept him from working on the house.

He hadn't meant to be rude to Ellie. The truth was it bothered him to have her near, although he had no idea why. She'd been kind to Sarah and good with Ethan. Why should it upset him that she had entered his house and won the hearts of his sister and his son?

He put away the clean dishes and filled up his water glass again. It had been hot working on the roof, but if he hadn't finished it now, he would have suffered worse temperatures as the summer lengthened.

Ellie hadn't agreed not to come back, he realized with sudden awareness. A small smile played on his mouth as he thought of her stubbornness. He had to make sure he sent her on her way if she returned. If she didn't listen, he would go to the bishop as she'd suggested.

Reuben continued to wonder how to handle Ellie Stoltzfus if she came back as she all but promised. Then his chest tightened with loss as he went into the gathering room to check on his sleeping son. It was wrong to notice another woman when his wife and the mother of his child, his precious Susanna, was dead.

Chapter Three

On Monday, Ellie returned to the Miller house to teach Sarah how to cook. "You'll need a large stockpot. I saw one in that bottom cabinet," she said, gesturing.

Sarah opened a door and grinned. "Here it is."

"*Gut.* First, we'll put in the chicken, then cover it with water. I bought chicken breasts because it's easier. You can use a whole chicken, but then you'd have to remove the meat from the bones. With the whole chicken, however, you'd get delicious chicken stock. I went to Whittier's and bought a container of chicken broth, which is easier and just as tasty. Just add a couple of tablespoons of the granules to the pot while you cook the chicken." She regarded Sarah with a pleased smile as she followed instructions.

The teenager beamed at her. "What next?"

Ellie went on to explain what other ingredients were necessary in making chicken corn chowder. Sarah followed her directions to the letter, then reduced the gas flame under the pot. She stood back and grinned. "I can remember that," the girl said.

"*Ja,* you can," Ellie said with approval.

"Now what?"

"I brought all the ingredients for making a straw-berry pie." She handed Sarah a recipe card. "Follow these instructions and you'll do fine." It was getting late. Ellie looked at her watch. "I need to get home." She had come well past noon after cleaning for the Brodericks. Reuben would be home from work soon and she didn't want him to find her here. She picked up her cell phone from the counter as she got ready to leave. She stared at Sarah a long moment. "Do you have paper and pencil? I want to give you my cell phone number. If you need me for any reason, call me. Will you do that?"

"*Ja*, I promise," Sarah said. "There's a pay phone across the road."

"*Gut.*" Ellie finished writing her name and cell phone number, then handed the paper to Sarah. "I hope Reuben enjoys his supper."

"He will." Sarah followed her to the door. "*Danki*, Ellie."

"'Twas my pleasure, Sarah."

"Will you come back to clean next week?"

Ellie agreed, then left the house. Reuben had pulled his buggy into the yard. Her heart started to race as he approached her. He didn't look happy. His mouth was tight and his eyes were cold.

"I told you that I didn't want you to clean house for us."

"I didn't clean." She lifted her chin as she glared at him. "I came to see Sarah." And his son.

He blinked. The tension left his expression and his blue eyes warmed slightly. "Have a nice night, then, Ellie."

Heart beating hard, she gave a jerk of a nod, then

climbed into her pony cart and left. As she drove home, her thoughts went to Reuben, who'd surprised her. He didn't mind her visiting his sister? Apparently not. As long as she didn't clean. She could work with that, she decided. She wanted to be there for Sarah and Ethan. She'd visit early in the day if she could. If the house became a little cleaner while she was there, then all the better. Ellie frowned. She had a feeling that Reuben would make sure the place stayed spotless, even if he didn't get enough sleep.

She sighed and turned her thoughts to her parents. She'd be home in time to help Mam with supper. When she drove into the barnyard fifteen minutes later, Ellie smiled. She waved to her father, who was in the yard with Jeremiah, his beloved dog. She'd been shocked when Dat had decided to get a dog. Her sister Nell, the animal lover of the family who was married to a veterinarian, must have had more influence on their father than the family had realized.

Ellie heard Jeremiah bark as she climbed out of the buggy. Her father approached with his dog on his heels. "Dat," she greeted. "Taking Jeremiah for a walk?"

"Ja." Dat regarded her with affection. "You're home early."

She nodded. "Finished with the Brodericks, then went to the Millers, a new family in Happiness." Her lips curving, she said, "I was teaching Sarah Miller how to cook. She never had much of a chance to learn with older sisters who did most of the cooking."

Dat's brows furrowed. "The Millers?"

"Ja. An Amish family who recently moved into our church district." She glanced off into space, envisioning the vast amount of work that still needed to be done to

Reuben's house. "The family moved into that old English place we've passed and commented on."

"Do they need help with the renovations?"

"*Nay*, the owner seems determined to handle the work himself."

"If he changes his mind, I'll be happy to gather a crew to help out."

Ellie smiled as she bent to pet Jeremiah. "I'll tell him." When the dog lay down and rolled over for a tummy rub, she laughed. She crouched and gave him some attention. "Where's Mam?" she asked as she straightened.

"At Aunt Katie's."

"Shall I plan supper?"

"I'm sure your *mudder* will appreciate it."

She studied her father carefully. "You feeling *oll recht*, Dat?"

"I'm fine."

Ellie stared at him. She didn't believe it. She'd caught his grimaces of pain too often in the last couple of months. "I'll feed the animals first."

"I'll feed them," he said.

"But I don't mind."

"Fine. Jeremiah and I will finish our walk, then." That her father gave in so easily only confirmed that he wasn't feeling well. "Charlie's marrying soon," he said. "Someday you'll find a man you'll want to wed, too. What will I do without you?"

She placed a gentle hand on his shoulder. "Dat, not to worry. I have no plans to get married anytime soon."

"But you'll marry and have children someday, *ja*?"

"*Ja*, someday."

"*Dochter*, you're twenty-one. You don't have forever." He smiled. "And I wouldn't mind more grand-children."

"There's time enough," she insisted. "I'm not an old maid yet." After waving him on with his walk, she went inside to plan supper. She took chicken out of the freezer to thaw in the refrigerator for tomorrow. Ellie decided that tonight they'd finish the leftover roast beef. She'd make gravy so they could enjoy open-faced hot roast beef sandwiches. Then she made macaroni salad as a side dish before heading toward the barn to feed the animals.

Charlie pulled her pony cart into the barnyard as she crossed the yard. Ellie waved, and her sister grinned as she returned the wave. She jumped down from the cart, secured the horse, then joined Ellie, who stood watch-ing her with an affectionate smile.

"Going to feed the animals?" Charlie asked. "Want help?"

"I wouldn't mind it." It was June, and in just five short months, Charlie would marry Nate and move into the farmhouse he was currently renovating. She would miss her sister when she was gone. She'd be the only one left at home with their parents.

"I had the best day," Charlie said. "You should see what Nate's done to the house. I'm going to love liv-ing there. We'll have plenty of room for a big family."

Startled, Ellie turned to study her as they entered the barn together. "You want a big family?"

"I do. You know how much I love *kinner*."

"I know." Her sister had always had a soft spot for children. It was why she'd agreed to babysit for Nate's stepmother and why she'd been eager to teach at their

Happiness School. "I take it that Nate likes children, as well."

"Oh, *ja*! And he's so *gut* with them."

"A match made in heaven," Ellie murmured beneath her breath.

Her sister's sigh made Ellie grin. *"Ja."* Charlie filled up two feed bags and went to the horses first.

Ellie grabbed a bucket and filled it with chicken feed, then went out to toss the grain on the ground. As she watched the chickens peck at their food, Ellie heard her cell phone ring. Expecting one of her clients, she answered. *"Hallo?* This is Ellie."

"Ellie?" an anxious female voice said. "'Tis Sarah. Something happened. Can you come now?"

She knew instant fear. "I'll be right over."

"Danki," Sarah murmured and hung up the phone.

Ellie ran into the barn. "Can you finish with the animals? I just got a phone call and I need to go."

Charlie frowned. *"Ja*, of course. Is something wrong?"

"I don't know," she replied honestly.

Ellie ran to the pony cart. Within seconds, she steered her horse down the main road toward the Reuben Miller property. Had something happened to Ethan? Or Reuben? Fearful thoughts chased one another until the stress made her chest tighten.

No buggies were in the yard as Ellie drove up next to the house. She'd been gone only a short time. What had happened? She ran to the side door and it opened immediately, revealing a tearful Sarah.

"What is it?" Ellie asked with concern. "Is Ethan *oll recht*?"

Sarah bobbed her head. "Can you come inside?"

Ellie followed her into the kitchen and waited while

the girl calmed down enough to explain. "Sarah?" she prompted softly.

"Dat called and left a message. Something happened to my *mam*. He has asked me to come home."

"Oh, Sarah," Ellie said with sympathy. "Did he say what's wrong?"

"Nay." The teenager shook her head. "But I know he wouldn't ask unless it was important. He knows Reuben needs me."

"Do they want your *bruder* to come home, too?"

"Just me. I have to go. I'm sorry. You told me to call if I needed you," Sarah said. "I need you, Ellie. I need you to take care of Ethan while I'm gone."

The pain in Ellie's chest intensified. "Me?"

"Ja, he likes you. He quiets down whenever you hold him. *Please* watch him for me. Reuben needs to work. He won't make any money if he has to stay home." She blinked back tears. "Will you do it, Ellie? Will you take care of Ethan for me?"

Ellie swallowed hard as she considered Reuben's reaction. *"Ja,* I'll do it. I'll take care of Ethan for you. When do you have to leave?"

Sarah looked away. "A car is coming for me within the hour. I've already packed."

Shocked, Ellie could only nod. "What time is Reuben expected home?"

"I'm not sure. He left about an hour ago after learning about a problem at his current job site."

She glanced at her watch. "'Tis nearly supper time. Do you want me to fix you something to eat?"

"Nay. I'm not hungry." In her anxiety, Sarah clasped her arm. "The chicken corn chowder and strawberry pie I made are in the refrigerator for you and Reuben.

Promise me you'll take care of Ethan no matter what. I know my *bruder* can be difficult."

Ellie briefly closed her eyes. "I can handle Reuben."

"Then you promise?"

She nodded. "I promise I'll take *gut* care of your nephew."

Sarah released a sigh of relief. "*Danki*, Ellie. I'll get word to you as soon as I can."

"Should I stay here until Reuben gets back?"

"I don't know how long he'll be gone. If it's too long, you can leave, telling him that you have Ethan at your *haus*," the teen suggested.

Ellie thought for a moment. "I'll do that."

Sarah hugged her. "*Danki*, Ellie. You are a true friend."

A cry from the other room announced that Ethan was awake. "Go get your bag, Sarah. I'll take care of this little man." While the girl ran upstairs, Ellie went into the gathering room, where Ethan sat up in his cradle. She picked him up and cuddled him. The smell of his diaper told her it needed changing.

"Well, little one…'tis you and me for a while. Let's fix your problem, then we'll spend some time together, *ja*?" The little boy was a beautiful child who resembled his father. What was Reuben going to say after learning she'd agreed to babysit indefinitely for his son? The man hadn't wanted her to clean his house. She could imagine what he'd have to say about watching Ethan.

What have I gotten myself into?

She needed to get word to her parents about what had happened. Using her cell phone, she made a call to their neighbors and asked them to let her family know that she'd be home as soon as she could.

School currently wasn't in session. Perhaps Charlie could help with Ethan's care until Ellie figured out a way to make time from her cleaning schedule for babysitting.

Less than an hour later, Sarah left. Ellie waited another hour and a half for Reuben's return before deciding to head home with Ethan.

Before leaving, she bathed and powdered Ethan, then wrote Reuben a long note, explaining what had happened and where Ethan was. She'd made sure she'd packed a bag with diapers, a bottle and food for the new charge. She hoped Reuben wouldn't be too angry that she'd left with his son. But she felt that she and Ethan were better off at her parents', since she didn't know how long Reuben would be gone.

Dear Lord, please help Reuben understand why I've taken his son home with me.

It was late when Reuben made it home after dealing with a plumbing emergency in the house they'd been building. He'd shut off the water, then had to figure out a way to clean up the mess while salvaging whatever he could in the rest of the house for his employer and the future homeowner.

It was close to nine when he drove his buggy into the yard. When he'd left the house earlier, he'd met an English driver hired by the construction company to transport their Amish crews. Reuben, newly promoted to foreman on this job site, had discovered that the plumber had failed to check his apprentice's work before leaving for the day. The flood of water from an improperly connected pipe had done an undeterminable amount of damage.

His body ached from stress as he climbed out of his vehicle and went inside. The house was silent, but he expected it to be. Ethan would have been put to bed earlier, and Sarah was probably in her room reading or fast asleep.

It was nearly dark outside and pitch-black inside, so he felt his way to the drawer where he kept a flashlight. He clicked on the light before he washed his hands at the kitchen sink and splashed water on his face. He was exhausted. The only thing he wanted to do was climb into bed and sleep for as long as possible before meeting up with his boss the next day.

After drying his hands and face with a towel, he tossed it into the washing machine in the back room. When he returned to the kitchen, he spied a piece of paper on the dining table. He read the note, then growled with frustration. His son and sister weren't at home. Sarah was no longer in Happiness. She'd gone to Ohio, summoned by their father. Ethan was with Ellie Stoltzfus at the woman's house. Ellie had written that she thought it best to take Ethan there to wait for his return. If he came in late, he shouldn't worry about coming to get him. She'd bring him home first thing in the morning. She knew he'd been working hard and he needed his rest.

Reuben growled with frustration. Ellie Stoltzfus had his son? He wasn't about to leave him with the Stoltzfuses. And he needed to know more of what had happened.

He sank into a chair to catch his breath and to summon the energy to get moving again. He scowled when he thought of Ellie and her nerve in taking *his* son home with her.

Anger gave him impetus, and he rose and grabbed

his flashlight. He got back into his buggy and headed out to get his son. He'd have a few choice words with Ellie. He was more than annoyed. Having to make this trip was the last thing he needed, but he wanted his son safe and at home.

What was he going to do about Ethan now that Sarah was gone?

Reuben knew he had to find a wife and quickly. But first he had to contend with Ellie Stoltzfus and get the full story from her.

Chapter Four

After a last check that Ethan was asleep in a crib in her bedroom, Ellie headed downstairs. It was late and dark out. Was Reuben still dealing with trouble at work? Had he gone home and found her note?

She went into the kitchen to find her mother heating milk on the stove.

"He all settled in?" Mam asked.

"Ja." She bit her lip.

"Want a cup of sweetened warm milk?"

Ellie nodded. She felt terrible that she hadn't told her parents previously about cleaning house for Reuben Miller. She'd been afraid to mention him, considering what had happened between him and her sister Meg. Since arriving with Ethan, she had confessed everything. "Mam…"

Mam met her gaze. "Elizabeth Stoltzfus, I know what you're going to say," she scolded. "Don't you dare apologize for not telling us about Reuben. I understand your concern, but you're wrong. Dat and I have always liked Reuben. He was wonderful with Meg after the accident."

"An accident he caused," she pointed out.

"The accident wasn't his fault. The fault, if anyone's, belonged to the Englisher who hit Reuben's buggy, then left."

"They never found out who drove the car," Ellie murmured.

"*Nay*, but it doesn't matter. Meg and Reuben are both fine. Meg is happy with Peter and being mother to little Timothy." Her mother smiled. "Reuben moved on, as well."

Ellie nodded. "But life hasn't treated him as kindly. His wife died only minutes after giving birth to that precious little boy in my room."

"Is Reuben angry with his son?"

Ellie smiled, remembering the love in his gaze as Reuben had held his son. "*Nay*. He's a *gut vadder*. He loves Ethan."

Her mother filled three mugs of hot milk, then added sugar to each one. One for each of them and one for her father. "He's a fine man. I'm glad you can help him."

She was glad, too, but she doubted Reuben was. From what she'd encountered from him so far, he resented help—at least he did hers. He'd be here as soon as he read her note. He'd be angry, but she wouldn't apologize. She'd done the right thing in bringing Ethan home with her.

Ellie decided to drink her milk on the front porch. She murmured good-night to her parents, then took a seat in a rocking chair outside. How long before Reuben's arrival? For he would come. And he wouldn't be happy when he did.

It was a pleasant night. The stars were out in full force, bright lights twinkling in a midnight sky. She caught sight of a shooting star and, despite her worries, she felt a moment's contentment. There was something wonderful in caring for a child. Ethan Miller was precious, and she loved spending time with him. The fact that he took to her quickly made her feel special and loved. She was able to quiet him easily when he was tearful. He clung to her as if she were his mother and not a stranger.

Ellie set her empty cup down next to her chair and closed her eyes, then continued to rock. She'd been cleaning houses for years. She wanted a husband and children, but she couldn't worry about that now, for she had her parents to think about. She would keep up her business until Charlie married, save her money for when she'd need it.

She rocked back and forth in the chair until she got sleepy. A rumble in the yard startled her awake, and she recognized the man who pulled up his buggy close to the house. Ellie inhaled sharply. Time to face Reuben Miller. The man had come for his son.

She stood as she watched him approach the house. He didn't see her in the dark at first as he climbed the steps.

"*Gut* evening, Reuben," she said from the porch railing. She saw him stiffen.

"Ellie," he snapped, "where's Ethan?"

"He's upstairs sleeping," she replied quietly.

"I've come to take him home."

"I don't think that's wise, Reuben. He's settled in for the night. Why can't you let him sleep?"

"You had no right to take him."

She froze. "I didn't kidnap him, Reuben. I brought him here because I didn't know what time you'd be home. Didn't you see my note? I wrote that I'd bring him home in the morning."

"He needs to be home now."

She moved out from the shadows. The moon lent a glow to Reuben's face. She could read tension in his features, the pain of misunderstanding. "It's better if he's allowed to sleep." He looked exhausted, worried, and he probably needed the innocence of his baby son to ease his pain. She relented. "I'll get him for you."

His hand settled on her arm. "You're right," he said softly. "Don't wake him." He sighed. "'Tis been a long day. Do you mind if we sit a moment?"

"Please do." She softened toward him further. "Would you like something to drink? Hot cocoa or hot sweetened milk?"

He leaned back in the twin rocking chair and closed his eyes briefly. "Hot cocoa would be nice." He gazed at her, his expression stark and full of emotion. When she caught her breath, he closed off his emotions.

"I'll be just a moment." The water in the teakettle heated quickly. It took her but a moment to make him a cup of instant cocoa. She exited the house and handed him a mug, then sat down in the rocking chair. "It's instant."

He awarded her a slight smile. "It's perfect."

"Sarah left because something happened in Ohio," she said. "Your father sent a car. Whatever it was, your *dat* doesn't want you to worry. Sarah said she'd call tomorrow to let you know exactly what happened."

Reuben frowned. "As if I won't worry."

"I promised Sarah that I'd watch Ethan until her return."

He stiffened. "I'll stay home to take care of him."

"And miss work for how long?" She began to rock in the chair. His scent—earthy, male, pleasing to her sense of smell—reached out to her, intensifying her awareness of him. "I made your sister a promise, Reuben."

"And you always keep promises," he said bitterly.

"*Ja.* I do." She stifled her anger. "I know you don't want me at the house. If you prefer, I can ask Charlie to keep an eye on Ethan. She's *gut* with children. But I refuse to ask her to be at the house all the time, just because you have a problem with me personally. I will watch your son, so you might as well accept it." She paused. "I would never hurt Ethan."

He stared at her silently with eyes like sapphires in the dark. His gaze made her uncomfortable.

"Say something."

"What do you want me to say?" he asked. "You want me to admit that I don't want you in my *haus*?"

Ellie blanched at the direct hit. Ignoring the shaft of pain, she lifted her chin. "I don't care if you feel that way. It wouldn't change anything. I promised Sarah I'd take care of Ethan, and I will make good on that promise."

"With your sister," he said huskily.

She shrugged, though she felt anything but casual about the situation. "If necessary." She stood and went to the railing, giving him her back. "Since you seem fine with leaving your son here for the night, I'll make sure we get him home before you leave for work in the morning. Let's say by seven if not before. Will that work?"

He stood, handed her his empty mug. "*Danki* for the hot chocolate."

She nodded. "Reuben?"

The man released a tired sigh. "Seven tomorrow morning will be fine. No need to come earlier."

Without thought, Ellie placed a hand on his arm. She was shocked as she felt him tense, the muscle tightening. She withdrew quickly. He stared at her as if stunned that she'd touched him. A strange frisson of awareness cropped up between them.

Reuben looked away. "Good night, Elizabeth."

She watched him descend the porch steps and head toward his buggy. "Good night, Reuben," she murmured. He must have heard her, for he stopped and gazed at her for several long seconds before he climbed into his vehicle and left for home.

The next morning before seven, Ellie steered the buggy toward the Reuben Miller house. Charlie sat beside her holding Ethan. She flashed her a glance. "Are you sure you don't mind watching him this morning?"

"Not at all. You know I love children, and this little one," she said with affection, "is a sweetheart."

Ellie smiled at her sister. "I have one house to clean this morning. It won't take me long before I can relieve you."

"That's fine. I promised Nate I'd stop by to check on the progress of the farmhouse." Charlie grinned. "I'm excited to marry Nate. I never thought I'd ever be this happy," she confessed softly.

"You've liked him for a long time. It took him a while to see you for who you are." She recalled the difficulty the two had had getting together. "You're meant to be with him. You love him."

"I do." Charlie shifted Ethan so he could look out

the window as Ellie turned onto Reuben's driveway. "Look, Ethan! There's your *dat*!"

The child made a sound of pleasure as he recognized his father. Ellie pulled the buggy close to the side door, where Reuben waited.

She climbed out and took Ethan from Charlie until her sister alighted and reached for the little boy. "*Gut* morning, Reuben," she greeted.

He nodded, his expression sober, until his gaze settled softly on his son. "Was he any trouble?" he asked Charlie.

"None," Ellie said tautly, refusing to be ignored. "He slept through the night and I fed him before we left the *haus*."

He studied her briefly as Charlie handed him his son. "Ethan," he murmured, his eyes soft, as he took him into his arms.

"Reuben," Charlie greeted as she skirted the buggy with a smile. "I hadn't realized that you moved into our district."

Ellie waited for his expression to darken, but to her shock, he grinned. "I have a lot of work to do to this place yet, but 'tis home." She watched her sister and Reuben converse easily. Hurt, she turned and climbed into the buggy. Why didn't he like her? Why was Charlie acceptable as Meg's sister but not her? Her attention skimmed over him briefly before she addressed her sister. "I'll see you later, Charlie." To her relief, her sibling nodded without saying another word.

"Have a *gut* day," Reuben told her gruffly, almost reluctantly. Then, dismissing her, he kissed his son on the forehead before he waved Charlie toward the house. "Come in, and I'll show you around."

Swallowing against a suddenly tight throat, Ellie picked up the leathers, then left, heading to the Broderick household, her first and only cleaning job of the day.

The Broderick house was in the opposite direction from her house, but Ellie didn't mind the drive. The weather was nice and she needed the time to relax. Her brief encounter with Reuben had agitated her. That he could be so friendly to Charlie and not to her bothered her. A lot.

She drove up the Broderick driveway and parked her buggy near the garage. She tied her horse to the handle of the garage door, then grabbed her cleaning supplies before heading toward the house.

Ellie climbed the stoop and knocked on the glass outer door. Within seconds, the door opened, revealing Olivia Broderick. "Mrs. Broderick," she murmured in greeting.

Without a word, Olivia opened the door for her. Her gaze shot past Ellie to where she'd parked the buggy. "I don't want you parking your horse in the driveway," she said. "If he takes a dump on my pavers, you'll have to clean it up."

Ellie nodded. "Is there someplace else you'd like me to park?"

The woman sniffed. "I'd rather you not park anywhere near our property."

"Where, then?"

"I don't care, Eleanor," she said with disdain. "Just not here."

Drawing a calming breath, Ellie nodded. Her name wasn't Eleanor, but the woman continued to call her that whenever she was unhappy with her. Why had she

agreed to continue working for these people? Did she
need their money that badly?

"Upstairs today?" Ellie asked.

Olivia nodded. "The boys' rooms are a mess. If you
could start with them, then head down to the main floor,
that would be great."

Nodding, Ellie headed toward the stairs and climbed
to the second floor, fearing what she'd find once she
entered the woman's sons' rooms. In one room there
were clothes scattered across the floor. She stared at
them, then left the room and headed to a second bedroom. The floor was clean, the room tidy. She dusted
the furniture, then went into a hall closet to get out the
vacuum cleaner. After she vacuumed the rug, she put
it away, then headed downstairs.

"That didn't take long," Olivia said.

"I did your youngest's room. Your other son's floor is
covered with clothes. I clean houses," she said. "I don't
do maid service or laundry."

The woman narrowed her gaze at her. "Perhaps you'd
prefer to work someplace else."

"If you'd like." Ellie took her cleaning supplies and
headed toward the door.

"Wait."

Ellie stopped and turned. She had a feeling that no
one else would work in the house, that Olivia had never
expected that Ellie—an Amish woman—would dare
walk away from a job. "Yes?"

"If you leave," the woman said with a dark smile, "I
won't ask you back."

A harsh laugh escaped from Ellie's lips. "Have a
good day, Mrs. Broderick." Then she exited the house,

feeling better about her day as she stowed her supplies on the backseat.

"Wait!" The woman had followed her outside.

Ellie turned and watched the woman's approach, her gaze anxious.

"I'm sorry," Olivia said. "I..." She blinked, looking devastated. "Please stay. I need your help. I'm sorry I've been grouchy. I just learned I have cancer." She bit her lip. "*Please.* You don't have to do John's room. Will you finish the rest of the house?"

Heart welling with compassion, Ellie softened toward her. "Yes, I'll finish." She grabbed her supplies from her buggy and turned...and saw gratitude in the other woman's expression. She followed Olivia into the house and went right to work.

Ellie finished the Brodericks' home by eleven thirty and headed to the Miller house to relieve Charlie. In the end, she'd gone ahead and cleaned John's room. How could she not? But to her surprise, Olivia Broderick had picked up the clothes and put them in a laundry basket while Ellie cleaned her son Robert's room. As she steered the buggy down the road, she felt pleased with how well her morning went. Before she left, she promised to clean for Olivia toward the end of next week.

The woman had apologized more than once for her behavior. Ellie learned that she had just started her chemotherapy treatments, and Olivia confessed she already felt weak. Ellie couldn't imagine dealing with cancer or the long road ahead that Olivia faced. If she could help in any way, Ellie decided, she would be there for the woman. It was the least she could do when the Lord had blessed her with so much.

She caught sight of the Miller house and smiled. She

would pray for Olivia Broderick. And she would live in the moment, enjoying little Ethan, who had quickly captured her heart.

Reuben was bone-tired. After a long day of work yesterday followed by a sleepless night, he felt exhausted. Alone with Ethan, how would he get any rest? He loved his son, enjoyed every moment he had with him, but today he felt awful. He worried that he wouldn't be the kind of father he should be.

He hadn't heard from Sarah. Had she called while he was gone? He was worried. It wasn't like his parents to call her home at a time they knew he needed her. Had something happened to his father? His mother?

"*Hallo!* I'm home!" he called as he entered the house through the side door. "Anyone here?"

Carrying Ethan on her hip, Ellie entered the kitchen from the great room. Expecting Charlie, he was taken aback to see her.

She smiled at him. "*Hallo*, Reuben, did you have a *gut* day?"

"What are *you* doing here?" he demanded.

"I'm watching Ethan, like I told you I would."

"I thought you had to work today." He heard the harshness in his tone and wondered why she brought out the worst in him. Because he found her attractive and didn't want to?

"I finished the job this morning. When I was done, I came to relieve my sister." Her eyes narrowed, as if daring him to complain. "Is my presence here a problem?"

"*Ja,*" he bit out, then felt terrible when her face fell. "*Nay,*" he revised. "'Tis not a problem. I know you take good care of Ethan…"

"Then why are you so angry with me?" she whispered.

He shook his head, unable to explain, and the sight of her blinking back tears floored him. "I'm sorry. I've had a lousy day. I shouldn't have taken it out on you." He gave her a gentle smile. "Will you forgive me?"

Ellie appeared surprised, then her expression softened with understanding. "I know what it's like to have a bad day," she murmured. Ethan shifted in her arms and patted her cheek with his chubby little hand. She grinned and ran a finger across his baby-soft cheek. "Are you hungry?" she asked Reuben.

"I could eat," he said. A funny feeling settled in his chest as he watched the two of them.

"Have you tasted the chicken corn chowder Sarah and I made yesterday? And there's strawberry pie."

He blinked, shook his head. "I didn't know there was soup and pie." He studied her through tired eyes. "I guess I've been too tired to look. You taught her how to make my favorite meal."

"Sarah made the pie. I just gave her the recipe."

His chest tightened and his heart pumped hard as he gazed at her. "I haven't been home much lately." He suddenly realized that he hadn't gone grocery shopping. There had been only sandwich fixings and a few breakfast foods left in the house. "You must have bought groceries. How much do I owe you?"

"Nothing." Ellie dismissed his concern. The room lit up with the warmth of her smile. "I picked up a few things but the rest I brought from home."

"Ellie—"

"Reuben, if you want to buy some groceries yourself, I can make a list for you."

She placed his son in his arms, as if she were the boy's mother and had done it many times in Ethan's young life. He didn't want to think about the implications of his thoughts. As he held and jostled Ethan, Reuben watched as Ellie opened the refrigerator and pulled out a bowl. Next she ladled a measure of the bowl's contents into a pan she took out of the cabinet. She then set it on the stove and turned on the heat. Watching her work, he was glad that the gas stove was new—it was the first thing he'd bought for the kitchen when he'd moved in three weeks ago.

As the soup warmed, Ellie turned toward him with a smile. "Would you like crackers with your soup?"

He stared at her, transfixed. "We have crackers?"

She laughed. "*Ja*, there are oyster crackers. Sarah mentioned that you liked them."

Reuben scowled. "What else did Sarah say?"

"That you're a pleasant fellow mostly," she quipped, her smile lingering.

He opened his mouth to retort, but her good humor made him grin as she turned and pulled out an iced tea pitcher from the refrigerator.

"I made sun tea," Ellie said. She poured him a glass, then reached out to caress Ethan's head. The brief maternal gesture affected him like a kick to his belly. "Soup should be ready soon." She held out her arms. "May I hold him while you eat?" She eyed him carefully. "You should sit. You appear about ready to keel over."

He wanted to argue with her but couldn't. She made him feel things he didn't want to feel. But how could he object to her babysitting when she was obviously good with Ethan?

She stirred the soup, then started to ladle it into a bowl she'd taken out of a top cabinet. "How much would you like? I know you're tired, but you need to eat to keep up your strength."

He'd been ready to tell her he wasn't hungry, but then he smelled her soup. The scent of chicken corn chowder wafted through the kitchen, and he suddenly had an appetite. His stomach growled.

She chuckled. "That hungry, *ja*?" She regarded him over her shoulder with a twinkle in her pretty blue eyes. She narrowed her gaze. "When *was* the last time you've eaten?"

"I had breakfast this morning. A sausage sandwich from Whittier's Store. I ate it in the car on the way to the job site."

"You didn't eat lunch?" she scolded.

Instead of annoyed, he found himself amused. "I had a bag of pretzels and a bottle of cola around midday."

She made a *tsk* sound. "Reuben, you need to eat better or you'll get sick."

He arched an eyebrow at her, and she blushed. "Sorry," she mumbled.

She turned her attention back to his soup bowl, setting it on the kitchen table, out of Ethan's reach. Then she opened the box of oyster crackers before reaching for Ethan.

He studied her a long moment, and she reddened. Was she feeling it, too? he wondered as he gave her Ethan. This odd tension between them?

Ethan whimpered as Ellie cradled him with his head on her shoulder. She soothed him with a kiss on his forehead and gentle rubbing down his neck and back.

Reuben stared at her, his soup untouched. He tried to

imagine Susanna with their son but couldn't. He could only see Ellie, which made him feel angry and as guilty as if he'd sinned.

She froze, probably sensing his mood, and faced him. "You don't like your soup?"

"I haven't tried it yet."

A light furrow settled between her eyebrows. "Why not?"

He shrugged, then dipped his spoon for a taste. Reuben hummed with pleasure. The chicken corn chowder was delicious. He couldn't remember the last time he'd enjoyed a bowlful. He didn't think Susanna had ever made it for him. He'd eaten it after they were married, but it was his mother who'd made the soup. In fact, his mother had done almost all of the cooking, with Susanna helping to clean up afterward.

He met Ellie's worried gaze and smiled. "'Tis so *gut. Danki.*"

She grinned, looked relieved. "You're *willkomm.* I enjoy cooking."

"You do?"

She narrowed her gaze. "You're surprised that I can cook?"

"I didn't think you had time to spend in the kitchen with your *haus*-cleaning business."

"I don't clean *haus* all day, Reuben. Or I wouldn't be here, would I? I worked this morning. One job only, which is how I prefer it. I may be asked to handle two jobs in a day, but it's on rare occasions that I agree."

He watched myriad emotions cross her face. "I see."

"I like to be available for my parents if they need my help."

Concern filled him. "Are they ill?"

"*Nay.* Nothing like that." She shook her head. "It just doesn't seem right not to pull my weight at home."

He'd been tired, but Ellie's soup had revived him. "Did you hear from Sarah today?"

"I'm afraid not." Without asking, she refilled his soup bowl. He didn't object. "I'm sure we'll hear from her soon." She smiled down at the child in her arms. "Do you own a high chair?"

"*Nay*, but I'll buy one tomorrow." His voice lowered. "I didn't think about it. I'm sorry."

Ellie looked at him. "What are you sorry for?" she said. "You have enough worries. We have an extra one at home that no one is using. Charlie can bring it with her tomorrow."

"I can buy one for my son," he said sharply, then looked away, immediately regretting his tone.

"I know you can," she agreed. "Why don't you borrow ours until you find the time to buy one?"

His lips firmed but he kept silent. He didn't want her chair. He could buy or make Ethan a chair.

Ellie left the room. He'd sensed when she stiffened and felt the tension emanating in the air. Closing his eyes, he sighed. He was overwhelmed with emotion that confused him. What was it about this woman that made him feel this way?

Chapter Five

With Ethan on her hip, Ellie went into the great room to grab the quilt that had been draped over a chair. Why was Reuben so determined not to accept her help? She understood that he was a man trying to come to grips with all of the changes in his life. But he was making things difficult for himself, and she didn't understand why.

Back in the kitchen, she spread the quilt on the floor before settling Ethan close to Reuben. She'd cleaned the floor earlier, adding a layer of floor wax to smooth out the rough spots. She grabbed a wooden spoon from a drawer and handed it to the boy to play with.

She straightened and found Reuben watching her. He didn't say a word about her choice of toy for Ethan. She was relieved when the odd level of awareness between them dissipated as he consumed his second bowl of soup.

There was still chowder left in the pan. She set it on a hot mat. When it cooled, she'd store the rest in the refrigerator. She knew the soup was good, as it was her mother's recipe, rich in chicken, corn, noodles and vegetables. She recalled Sarah's enjoyment in learning to cook. Thoughts of Reuben's sister sparked her concern. Why hadn't Sarah called as promised? What had happened that her *dat* needed to send for her?

She faced Reuben, who was eating a cracker. "There's some soup left in the pan. Would you like more?"

He met her gaze. "*Nay*, I've had plenty. *Danki*. 'Tis *gut*."

Ellie found herself lost in his light blue eyes. "You've enough left for a couple of meals."

Reuben nodded but didn't comment. She checked on Ethan as she retrieved Reuben's empty bowl. She saw with a smile that the child was chewing on the tip of the wooden spoon. Aware of Reuben's study, she met his gaze. "I'll buy you another spoon."

His lips quirked with amusement. "He won't hurt it."

She felt her heart skitter in her chest as she noted his tender expression as he watched his son. The man was a good father. Had he been a good husband? She imagined he had been kind and loving to his wife.

The dark circles under his eyes told her how tired he was. Would he be able to sleep with Ethan in the house? Dare she offer to take him home with her?

She drew a steadying breath. "Reuben." When she encountered his gaze, she felt her attraction toward him like a shock to her system. "I don't mean to interfere, but I was wondering…would you like me to take Ethan home tonight so that you can sleep?"

His features tightened. "He's my son."

He'd reacted as she feared he would. "*Ja*, I know," she said quietly. She started to wash the dishes.

"Ellie." His soft voice and presence behind her gave

her a jolt. His hand settled gently on her shoulder and turned her to face him. "I'm sorry."

"I'm not trying to keep him from you," she whispered. Her throat tightened and she fought tears. Her shoulder tingled where his fingers touched her.

"I know." He released her suddenly as if he'd just realized that he'd been touching her. He ran a hand through his thick blond hair. "If you don't mind taking him home with you for the night, I'd appreciate it." He sighed heavily. "I'm well beyond tired."

She eyed him with warmth. "Charlie can bring him home before you leave for work in the morning."

Reuben nodded agreeably. *"Danki."* His brow furrowed. "What time will you be done with work tomorrow?" he asked.

"About eleven," she said. "Why?"

"I'm planning to work around the *haus* tomorrow. If Charlie doesn't mind watching him at home, you can bring him here with you after you've finished work."

"I'm sure Charlie won't mind watching him," Ellie said easily, but inside her heart raced wildly. He wanted her to bring him home? Why the sudden shift in attitude? "Depending on how the morning goes, I could be as late as one. Will you need me to stay and watch him?"

He inclined his head. *"Ja.* If you don't mind."

She flashed him a smile. "I don't mind." She grinned at Ethan, who played happily with his spoon. She looked up, met Reuben's gaze with a lingering smile. She glanced away after she noted the man's shuttered expression. "I'll finish the dishes and then we'll leave." She bit her lip. "If you still want me to take Ethan."

"Ja."

She felt glad that he trusted her enough to take Ethan

home. She took out the cold strawberry pie and spun to face him. "Would you like dessert?"

He grinned. "*Ja*, please."

Ellie cut him a huge slice and placed it on a plate with a fork. His face lit up like a little boy's when she set the dessert before him. "Enjoy."

She bent, picked up Ethan—spoon still in the baby's hand—then placed the boy on her hip. He fussed when she gently took away his spoon until she gave him a piece of mashed strawberry. "I'll pack Ethan's bag and then we'll leave," she said.

"*Danki*, Ellie." The warm look in his eyes made her breath hitch.

She climbed the steps to Ethan's room and packed his bag before she returned to the kitchen. Her cell phone rang, jarring the silence, as Ellie entered the room. Her gaze met Reuben's briefly. She gave him Ethan before she answered it. *"Hallo?"*

"Ellie?"

She immediately recognized Reuben's sister. "Sarah!" Reuben straightened and stared. "How are things in Ohio? We've been worried while waiting for you to call. What happened?"

Reuben stood and approached. "May I talk with her?" he mouthed.

She nodded. "Sarah? Reuben is here. I'll put him on."

"*Danki*, Ellie," he said as she handed him the phone. He flashed her a grateful smile.

"Sarah? What happened? Are Dat and Mam *oll recht*?"

Ellie tried not to eavesdrop during his conversation with his sister, but she couldn't help herself. She was curious and more than a little concerned. She reached for Ethan, and Reuben handed her his son without hesitation. She smiled at the little boy and took a seat at the table with Ethan on her lap. She waited patiently for Reuben to finish his call. Finally, he ended the conversation and handed back her phone.

"What happened?"

Reuben ran his fingers raggedly through his blond hair. "My *mudder* fell. She broke her arm and sprained her ankle. There is no one but Sarah to help her while she's recovering. It could be weeks before Sarah can come home." He hesitated. "My sister told my *eldre* that you're watching Ethan." His smile was apologetic. "I'm sorry, Ellie. 'Tis not right to impose on you. I'll look for someone to watch him for me."

"Why?" she said evenly. "I like spending time with Ethan—and so does Charlie. 'Tis no imposition to care for your son. Don't be in such a hurry to find another babysitter. I love spending time with him."

Warmth flickered in his light blue eyes. "Ellie…"

"Honestly, Reuben. 'Tis fine. Please don't worry about this." She stood and shifted Ethan to her hip before she retrieved the bag of the child's belongings from the table. "Do you want anything else to eat?"

"I'm stuffed." The warmth left his features, which suddenly became unreadable.

Ellie ignored his expression. "There are muffins in the pantry," she said. "I made them this afternoon so they'll still be fresh in the morning." She paused and attempted to gauge his thoughts. "I'll bring Ethan when I'm done. Or if you'd rather, Charlie can bring him first thing."

"*Nay*, after you've finished work is fine." He followed her toward the door. "I owe you, Ellie."

She stared, then scowled at him. "You owe me nothing, Reuben, so get that idea out of your head right now." Irritated, she swung open the door.

"Elizabeth," he murmured. "I didn't mean to upset you."

She froze and saw regret on his face. "I'll see you tomorrow," she said softly. "Get some rest. You look like you need it."

His lips twitched. "Is that a polite way of telling me I look awful?"

"Maybe." She returned his smile. He would never look terrible, she thought. He was too handsome and way too attractive to ever look bad to her. Shocked by her musings, she still managed to keep her expression neutral. "Sleep well, Reuben." Then she left and was conscious of his regard as he stood in the doorway while she climbed into her buggy and settled his son on her lap. With a wave, she led the horses out of the driveway and headed home.

Ethan was a sweet-natured baby. That night he settled in easily in the crib in her room, for which Ellie was grateful. After checking with her sister about watching Ethan in the morning, she decided to read awhile before getting ready for bed.

Early the next morning Ellie received a call from the client she was to clean for that day. Anita Moss had unexpected company for the week. Would Ellie clean for her after her guests left, next Thursday or Friday? Ellie told her she'd call to confirm the date after she checked her schedule. Then she gathered Ethan, who'd clung to her since he awakened, fed him, then started the drive back to the house.

* * *

Reuben woke at dawn after a good night's sleep, ate breakfast, then began to paint the interior walls of the first-floor rooms. After two hours he'd finished two coats on the kitchen and smaller rooms, then he moved on to work in the great room. The freshly painted walls made a difference, and he was pleased with the effect. A short time later, he eyed his handiwork in the second room with satisfaction. Ellie wasn't due to arrive yet with his son. The smell of paint would be nearly gone by the time they came. Next, he would tackle the bedrooms upstairs.

Reuben opened the kitchen windows before taking a breather outside with a glass of iced tea. He sat on the steps and studied the yard as he sipped from his glass. There was still so much junk in the back of the house. His stomach tightened as he envisioned the work entailed in getting rid of it—a rusted hollowed-out shell of an automobile. Two metal barrels that looked worse than the car, and too many other items in the back of the barn as well as inside.

And Ethan needed a high chair. He was ashamed that he hadn't thought of getting one before now. Sarah had fed Ethan while holding him. It was true his son was getting older, but did he have the money that would allow for the purchase of the chair? He had no idea how much one cost, but the last thing he wanted was to accept charity from the Stoltzfuses.

The sun felt warm but not overly so this morning. He finished his tea, set his glass aside, then leaned back on his arms and closed his eyes. A light breeze caressed his skin, and he could hear the sounds of nature. A bird in a nearby tree. The rustle of leaves. The sound of his own even breathing.

The spin of buggy wheels on his driveway had him opening his eyes. Charlie Stoltzfus steered the vehicle to a stop a few feet from where he sat. He stood as Ellie climbed out with Ethan in her arms. He saw Ellie lean into the carriage to talk briefly with her sister before she straightened and turned in his direction.

"*Hallo*, Reuben!" Charlie called with a wave and a smile. Then she left, leaving Ellie at the house without a way to get home.

He watched her approach. Ellie met his gaze and the smile left her face as she hesitated. "Reuben," she said cautiously.

"You're here early," he replied without emotion. He wasn't ready to see her. He'd wanted to finish inside the house before she and Ethan arrived.

"*Ja,*" she murmured. "I didn't have to work today."

"I didn't expect you until later."

Her mouth tightened. "Is there a problem?" she asked tartly.

Before he could explain, Ethan squealed with delight and extended his arms toward his father. His expression softening, Reuben reached for his son, and Ellie handed him the baby.

She stepped back to allow them time together. As he cuddled Ethan, he shifted his gaze to the woman who'd cared for his child during the night. She looked as if she felt she shouldn't be there.

"How was he through the night?" he asked, surprised by the huskiness of his voice.

Appearing to relax, Ellie smiled as she studied Ethan. "He was a *gut* boy. Fell asleep immediately when it was time for bed and slept through the night." She raised her eyes to meet his. "Did you sleep well?"

Reuben nodded. He had slept once he finally stopped thinking. He'd gotten up early to paint, but it had been worth it. He wondered how Ellie would react to the change. She stood a few feet away, looking uncertain. He shifted his son's weight to one arm.

"We'll have to stay outside for a little while," he told her.

She frowned. "Why? What's wrong?"

"Nothing. I painted the downstairs rooms this morning. I'd like them to air out a bit longer before we bring Ethan inside."

"Oh." Ellie looked relieved. "Are you pleased with how everything looks?"

"*Ja*, the rooms are white and clean."

"And you no longer need someone to come in to scrub them," she muttered.

He shot her a glance. "'Tis not about you, Ellie. 'Tis part of fixing up the *haus*. Painting is a part of the renovations. I need to replace the floor, as well."

She held his gaze silently as if to gauge his measure, then finally gave a nod. He moved on the step, giving her enough room to sit. Ellie hesitated, then took a seat next to him. They were silent. Reuben was aware of her clean scent and the warmth of her close proximity. He tried to concentrate on Ethan, but then his son reached for Ellie, drawing his attention back to the woman next to him. Reuben released him into her care. The sight of Ethan's chubby arms around Ellie's neck got to him, made him feel things he didn't want to feel. He stood abruptly. "Paint smell should be gone," he said.

He waited for Ellie to stand, then reached to open the door, letting Ellie and Ethan enter ahead of him.

She gasped as she caught sight of the room. "It looks beautiful. The bright walls make the kitchen look bigger." She shifted Ethan in her arms. "Did you say you did all of the first floor?"

He nodded. "The gathering room and the bathroom. I even painted the mudroom."

"You got a lot done." Her gaze narrowed. "I thought you said you slept."

Reuben grinned. He couldn't help himself. "I did, until right before dawn when I got up and decided this morning would be a good time to paint." He studied Ellie as she took in her surroundings. Today she wore a purple dress that brightened her pretty blue eyes. Her blond hair, more golden in color than his, was neatly pinned beneath her prayer *kapp*.

"I'd like to start painting upstairs this afternoon," he said. "Can you manage with staying downstairs with Ethan?"

Her lips firmed. *"Ja."*

He inclined his head. *"Gut."* He went to the refrigerator and looked inside. "Are you hungry? There is soup left."

"I wouldn't mind a small bowl." She handed Ethan back to him. "I'll fix lunch."

Reuben wanted to object. Ellie was already doing too much for him and Ethan, but he knew he would only upset her if he insisted on preparing the meal, so instead he sat on a kitchen chair and settled Ethan in his lap. His son smelled like baby powder and sunshine. He studied him a moment before focusing his gaze on Ellie. She'd taken good care of Ethan and he appreciated it. As much as it pained him to accept help, he knew he couldn't manage on his own. And she seemed to enjoy watching his boy…at least until Sarah returned. He frowned. If his sister returned.

He hoped Sarah would call soon to bring him up to date on his mother's injuries. Maybe he should have moved with his parents to Ohio, but Lancaster County had always been his home, and he hadn't wanted to leave it. He'd already suffered too many changes in his life. And with this house, there was a promise of a better future.

He watched Ellie dump the soup into a pan and set it on the stove. She didn't glance back as she turned on the gas burner and waited for the chowder to heat. Stirring the soup, she stared into the pot, obviously lost in thought.

"Ellie."

She startled, then faced him. *"Ja?"*

"I didn't mean to be rude this morning."

Her lips twitched. "You can't help yourself, I know."

He was shocked when he heard himself laugh. To his delight, Ellie chuckled. They shared a moment of amusement, but when it dissipated, awareness cropped up between them. Conscious of his attraction to her, he rose with Ethan, eager to escape her presence if but for a moment, and went into the great room to check on the drying paint. As he studied his handiwork, Reuben felt immense satisfaction for the way the paint had transformed the room's appearance.

Ethan patted his cheek, demanding his attention. Reuben gasped with exaggeration and his son giggled. He grew soft as he gazed at the little boy he and Susanna had made together. Life could have been near perfect, but her death had been like a kick in the teeth, which had made him reevaluate his circumstances. He blinked as emotion threatened to overwhelm him.

"Reuben, the soup's hot," Ellie called from the doorway and he turned. He heard her inhale sharply, her gaze intent on his features. "I'll take Ethan for you," she murmured softly. Then she left, as if she wanted to give him a few moments alone to compose himself.

Perceptive woman, he thought with a little smile as the dark sense of loss left him. Still, he didn't return to the kitchen immediately. He crossed the room to peer out the window, absently touching light fingers to the wall next to him and noticing that it was completely dry. He stared out into the front yard. The view was decent. He couldn't see the junk in the yard from here. Maybe he needed to tackle cleaning up the grounds next so Ethan could have a place to play. He'd build him a swing set. There were bills to be paid, but eventually he'd have enough money to buy the materials he'd need for swings.

His stomach growled, a reminder that he'd skipped breakfast. After a calming breath, Reuben felt peace settle over him. He entered the kitchen to see Ellie placing soup bowls on the table. Ethan sat on a quilt on the floor, playing with a wooden spoon. He studied his son and became amused when Ethan grinned at him, waved the spoon in the air, then put the tip of it in his mouth.

"It smells *gut*," Reuben said as he took his seat.

With a small smile, Ellie joined him at the table. "*Ach nay*, I forgot the crackers." She sprang to her feet.

He reached to stop her with a gentle hand on her arm. "No need to get them," he said quietly. "Unless you want some for yourself."

She shook her head. "We need drinks, though. Iced tea?"

He nodded. Their gazes locked and he became conscious that he held her arm. Her skin was soft and silky to the touch. Startled, he released her and focused on eating his soup. Ellie was silent as she poured two glasses of iced tea. He took a sip from the one she handed him.

"This tea is *gut*," he said with surprise. He drank more.

Ellie flushed with pleasure. "'Tis sun tea. The tea steeped in a large gallon jar I found in your pantry. I just filled it with water and some tea bags, then put it out in the sun to heat."

Reuben studied his glass before meeting her gaze. "It tastes sweet and has lemon in it."

She smiled. "While the tea was still hot from the sun, I added sugar and lemon."

"You know your way around a kitchen," he said with a smile.

Looking uncomfortable with his praise, she averted her glance. "Spent a lot of time in one."

Reuben watched her silently as she continued to eat. Eventually Ethan grew fussy.

Ellie jumped from her seat and scooped Ethan into her arms, and the wooden spoon fell to the floor. "What's wrong, little man, did you hit yourself with the spoon?" she murmured soothingly to him. "I'll rub it better for you." She smiled as she stroked the reddened area on his left leg. The child stopped crying and gave her a watery smile. "Are you hungry?"

"You'd make a *gut* mother," Reuben praised. He regretted the observation as soon as he caught her expression. "What I mean," he quickly added, "is that Ethan responds well to you." He'd instantly regretted his words. While Ellie might be the perfect mother for his son, his unwanted attraction to her compounded with his love for his late wife reminded him it was foolish to consider Ellie.

Chapter Six

Startled by his comment, Ellie was aware of Reuben's continued gaze on her as she cuddled his son. She would have thought he would blame her for Ethan's injury. After all, she'd given Ethan the spoon. But instead of complaining, he'd given her praise. Surprised, she couldn't look at him, preferring instead to focus on the child in her arms. Reuben already churned up enough odd feelings within her she found disturbing.

She hugged his son, smoothed a gentle touch across his sore thigh, then placed a kiss on his forehead. As Ethan laid his head on her shoulder, Ellie blew against his neck, the raspberry sound making him laugh. She grinned. The little boy giggled as she repeatedly blew against his neck until she was stopped by her own laughter.

Reuben stood, moved past her to put their empty bowls in the sink. Then he paused near her shoulder. She tensed but forced herself to meet his gaze. There was surprising warmth in his blue eyes. She relaxed briefly, only to become startlingly aware of the tension she felt. A soft smile curved the man's lips and suggested he enjoyed watching the interaction between her and Ethan. She returned his smile before bending to blow another kiss in the crease of his baby's neck.

Reuben ran a hand gently across her shoulder as he reached to tickle Ethan. Ellie's breath caught, but Ethan laughed, the merry sound infectious. She grinned. It felt wonderful to laugh. The little boy put his arms about her neck. When he placed his head on her shoulder, Ellie melted.

"Hey, little one," she said softly. "Feel better enough to eat?"

"What will you feed him?" Reuben asked.

"I brought a box of cereal."

"Dry cereal?" He looked surprised. "He can eat that?"

Her gaze went soft. "*Ja.* Didn't Sarah give him finger food?" She raised Ethan high and tickled him by rubbing her nose onto his belly. The boy giggled and clutched the top of her head, nearly pulling off her prayer *kapp*. Ellie gently caught the little hand in time.

Reuben was silent. He appeared troubled.

"Reuben?" she said softly. "What's wrong?"

"I don't know much about my son," he admitted with concern.

"You know enough." She hesitated. "You're a *gut vadder*. Ethan is happy and comfortable in your arms." She caressed the little one's cheek. "Children don't come with directions. We do the best we can." She smiled at him. "You've been working hard. You mustn't worry because you can't anticipate every one of Ethan's needs."

He stared at her with a frown. She saw emotion briefly flicker across his expression, then disappear. His demeanor changed. "I must get back to work," he said crisply.

Then he left the house so abruptly that she gaped at the back of him as he made his escape.

Minutes later, Ellie heard footsteps going upstairs. He must have come in the front door with whatever supplies he needed. She tried to forget the awkward moment between them, concentrating on Ethan instead. She hugged the boy close before setting him on the quilt and taking his cereal from a cupboard. Reuben needed a high chair for Ethan, but until he bought one, she'd sit at the table with the child on her lap. She poured a small of amount of cereal on the table within Ethan's reach and was rewarded when he grabbed and shoved a piece in his mouth.

After lunch, she laid him down for a nap in the great room, then washed and dried the lunch dishes. Once Ethan fell asleep, Ellie took a moment to sit quietly before planning supper for Reuben so that he had something to reheat when he was hungry.

It was late afternoon when Reuben finally came downstairs. He entered the kitchen, then stopped abruptly, as if he'd forgotten she was there. "What are you doing?" he asked politely. "Something smells delicious."

Warmed by the compliment, Ellie turned away from the stove to face him. "I made chicken potpie to reheat when you're ready. If you're hungry now, you can eat it while it's hot."

He looked tired as he ran a hand through his blond hair. "I just need a moment to clean up."

She managed a smile for him. "I'll ladle you a bowlful. I take it you like chicken potpie?"

He nodded. "*Ja*, although I haven't had any in…"

"Since your parents moved to Ohio?" she guessed.

His brows furrowed. "Much longer than that." He narrowed his gaze. "What do you know about my parents?"

She shrugged, ignoring his terseness. "Just what Sarah told me. That they moved to Ohio to live closer to your *mudder*'s *eldre*. Your sister stayed behind to help with Ethan."

Reuben was silent a long moment. "'Tis true." He sighed. "But I should have made her go. She's too young to take so much responsibility."

"She loves you and Ethan. She's happy to help."

He approached and stared into the pot while she stirred. "I need a wife," he murmured. "My son needs a mother."

Ellie tensed. She picked Ethan up and gave him to his father. "You want to fall in love and marry again?"

"*Nay*, I'll marry but I won't fall in love."

"You'd wed without love?"

"I'd wed for Ethan." He combed his fingers through Ethan's fine baby hair. "But love? *Nay*. I don't want or need it."

What woman would agree to such an arrangement? "I see." She glanced out the window to see her sister pulling the family buggy close to the house. Ellie reached for her satchel on the other end of the counter. "I have to go. Charlie's here."

It was important that she be on hand to help her mother. Soon Charlie would be married and it would be up to Ellie, the only daughter who'd be left at home, to make her parents' lives easier.

She felt Reuben watching her as she picked up her

bag, was conscious of him as he followed her out of the house. Charlie waved and called out to him. Ellie glanced back briefly to see Reuben wave back. She studied father and son. His arms circling Reuben's neck, Ethan was happy to be held by his father.

She stowed her bag in the back of the buggy, then climbed onto the front seat. With a last look in his direction as Charlie pulled away, Ellie wondered how a man who obviously loved his son could dismiss love in marriage so easily. What woman would be happy to be married to such a man and not fall in love with him? And with his son? Her thoughts in turmoil, Ellie was silent as they headed for home.

"You're quiet. Everything *oll recht*?" Charlie asked.

Ellie managed a smile. "*Ja,* Ethan and I had a *gut* day."

"I can watch Ethan for you tomorrow if you need me to."

"*Danki.*"

Early the next morning Ellie drove her sister to the Reuben Miller house before heading to her first cleaning job. Reuben had to work on a new construction site, and he needed someone to stay with Ethan. She longed to stay but couldn't. Her cleaning business would keep her occupied until noon, if not later.

"Are you sure you don't want to stay and watch Ethan?" Charlie asked as she eyed her knowingly.

"I can't," Ellie told her. "I've two jobs to do today, but I'll come as soon as possible to relieve you."

Charlie smiled. "I don't mind watching him for the day if you can't get away."

But I mind, Ellie thought. She wanted to spend time with the little boy. She loved Ethan. It was hard not to fall for the sweet, delightful child. She wished she could stay. She was fast losing her desire to clean house for Englishers, but until she gave it up after Charlie married, she had clients to keep happy. "I appreciate your help, Charlie." She changed the subject. "How are the *haus* renovations coming?"

Her sister grinned. "*Wunderbor!* Nate's been working hard on them while still helping his *dat* on the farm." A dreamy look entered her sister's expression. "I'm going to love living there."

"Especially with Nate," Ellie said with a grin.

Her sisters were blessed to have found good men they loved and respected. Someday, she hoped to be as blessed. She wanted a man who loved her. A husband who wanted to be her life's partner and raise a family with her.

Not everyone was as lucky in love, she thought with sadness. Reuben had loved and lost. He'd suffered so much that he couldn't bear marrying for love again. But he'd marry for Ethan.

Ellie could never marry a man who didn't love her. Even if the man was handsome, kind and a good father. Something shifted inside her breast. Reuben Miller possessed all the attributes of a good life partner. But he would offer friendship only. For herself, she wanted more.

Thank the Lord that she was immune to such a man.

The house loomed ahead. Ellie switched on the battery-run blinker before she steered her vehicle onto Reuben's driveway. The spare high chair that had been left unused in what had previously been Leah's bedroom was on the backseat. Charlie had insisted they bring it despite Reuben's objection, and Ellie wasn't going to argue with her sister. Would he be angry?

She parked the buggy and got out while her sister climbed out the other side. Charlie took out the chair. Ellie looked toward the house but didn't see Reuben.

"You look nervous. He really doesn't want this chair?" Charlie said knowingly.

Ellie released a heavy breath. "*Nay.* He doesn't." Her lips firmed. "But maybe you can convince him otherwise." She studied the chair. "Do you need help with it?"

"*Nay,* I can manage it on my own."

Ellie watched Charlie cart the chair up to the side door, then set it down on the stoop to knock. The door opened. Reuben flashed her sister a smile. He saw the chair and quickly reached out to take it from her. Charlie waved at her, and Ellie turned to leave, but not before catching the thunder in Reuben's expression.

"So you're angry with me and not Charlie?" Ellie murmured as she climbed into her vehicle. *Learn to live with it,* she thought as she picked up the leathers and steered the horse toward her first cleaning job of the day.

Reuben carried in the high chair. "Where do you want it?"

"Close to the kitchen table," Charlie said, watching with unreadable green eyes.

"What?" he said once he'd set up the chair.

"You're upset with my sister. She said you would be." The young woman regarded him thoughtfully.

"I told her that I didn't want it. I can buy a chair for my son."

Charlie nodded. "I understand, but why not use this

one until you do?" She left the room but came back within seconds with Ethan on her hip. "She didn't want to bring it and upset you, Reuben." She smiled at his baby as she buckled him into the chair and slid the tray close to his body. "I was the one who insisted."

Reuben felt his gut wrench. "You?"

She crossed her arms as she faced him. "*Ja*, me. Ellie wanted to honor your wishes, but I—we—need a place to keep him safe while we feed him. He's old enough to sit on his own."

"Charlie—"

"You owe her an apology," she said. "I don't understand why you dislike accepting help."

"I've accepted yours and Ellie's," he pointed out. "With Ethan."

Charlie gave him a smile. "*Ja*. You should probably get to work or you'll be late."

"I...*danki*, Charlie."

Her lips curved. "We'll take *gut* care of your son."

"I know." His heart ached with the mistake of misunderstanding. Reuben grabbed his hat and his tool belt, then waited outside for his ride. Today he would be working with Jed and Elijah Lapp—Ellie's cousins. He was still waiting on plumbing repairs on his other job. His crew was split up and working other sites until the repairs were finished.

Jedidiah arrived alone. Reuben approached the man's vehicle and greeted him with a nod. "Going to be a warm one, I'm afraid," Jed commented pleasantly.

"*Ja*, it is," Reuben agreed.

"Looks like you've got a lot of work to do here yet."

Reuben stiffened. *"Ja."*

"Let us know if you need a hand." The man met his gaze.

He nodded. "I will. *Danki*." But he wouldn't be asking for help. He had something to prove to himself—that he was capable of doing things on his own.

Jed steered his wagon onto the main road. "Heard you got a son."

"You heard right."

"Mam said my cousins have been watching him for you."

Reuben tensed. They were talking about him. "*Ja*, they have been."

Jed grunted. "*Gut.* They'll take *gut* care of him. Even guard him with their lives."

He went still until the man laughed. "Let's hope they don't have to," Reuben said with a chuckle.

The day went fairly quickly for Reuben, considering that the sun was hot and the labor hard. Jed had him home by four thirty. He climbed down from Jed's vehicle. "Appreciate the ride, Jed."

The man smiled. "Anytime. See you tomorrow."

He waited until Jed had left before he turned. He felt worn out from the heat as he approached the house. He was aware that his blue short-sleeved shirt was stained with sweat and his pant legs and shoes dusty with dirt from the job site. They were building a small shopping center between the villages of Bird in Hand and Intercourse. When it was finished, there would be room for three shops. All of them, according to Jed, would be Amish owned and run. While he had no desire to be involved in businesses that attracted tourists, he understood what these businesses meant to Amish families who wanted to make a good living. He preferred construction or farming.

Reuben tried to open the side door but it was locked. He frowned. Did one of the sisters take Ethan home with them? He rapped on the door and waited. He was in a lousy mood. The last thing he needed was to fetch Ethan. When no one answered his knock, he started to simmer. He knocked harder out of frustration. The door suddenly swung open, and he could hear a child's cry.

Ellie stood in the doorway and gazed at him with irritation. "You woke up Ethan, and I'd just gotten him to sleep."

He stared at her through narrowed eyes, but his anger vanished with the onset of relief. "'Tis nearly five."

The woman turned and walked away, leaving the door open for him to follow her. She went into the great room and drew Ethan into her arms, urged his head onto her shoulder, then rubbed his back to soothe his child. Ethan finally quieted and his eyelids drifted closed. "He's been fretful all afternoon. I hope he's not coming down with something."

Reuben approached and placed a hand on his son's forehead. "He's warm."

Ellie looked at him. "'Tis hot today. I don't think he has a fever."

He swallowed hard at the compassion and tenderness he saw on her features. Something moved deep within him. She was an astounding woman who would make some man a good wife and mother for his children someday.

Reuben looked away. He didn't want to notice anything about Ellie. She was a complication he didn't need. "How can I help?"

Her smile nearly stopped his heart. "There isn't much to do at this point. I'll hold and comfort him until he falls asleep again." Ethan opened his eyes and tried to lift his head. Ellie rubbed his neck, and he lay against her shoulder again.

"Do you need a break?" Reuben whispered. "I can hold him awhile."

"He's settled down some," she said softly. "Better not to move him." She regarded him with warmth. "Supper's ready for you. 'Tis just macaroni salad, sweet and sour green beans and some fried chicken I picked up on my way over this afternoon. Everything is in the refrigerator. Chicken is usually *gut* cold, but if you want, I can heat it up for you."

She carried Ethan carefully toward the refrigerator and opened the door.

"Ellie, I can get it."

She nodded, swung the door shut and stepped back. She looked hurt. He closed his eyes, wondering what to say to wipe that look from her eyes. "You've done so much and I appreciate it," he said softly. "Ellie—" She met his gaze. "I'm sorry for being stubborn about the high chair. Your sister said that it was her idea to bring it. I should have accepted your offer when you made it."

Ellie looked surprised yet glad. "You can give it back when you no longer need it."

"Your family doesn't need it?"

"Nay." She shifted Ethan in her arms. "Not anytime soon." She smiled at his little boy. "I think he's nodded off." Her voice was quiet, almost reverent. The beauty in her features arrested him, and he was forced to admit there was something compelling about her

that drew him in. Ethan was fast asleep with his head on her shoulder.

"Do you want to put him down?" he asked.

She shook her head. "Let's make certain he is asleep first. *Ja?*"

He nodded. "I'll get dinner ready. You'll join me once you put him down?"

Ellie blinked rapidly. "You want me to eat supper with you?"

"Ja." He searched her expression, saw her surprise. "Do you need to be home?"

"Nay. I like to help Mam, but Charlie's home so she can help her."

His relief startled him. *"Gut."*

Ellie was stunned. Reuben had invited her to stay to eat supper. The knowledge shook her. Earlier, he'd been angry with her. Was he trying to make amends?

His apology had shocked her. He'd said that he should have accepted her offer of the chair from the start. What an enigmatic man.

Ethan felt good in her arms. He smelled of baby powder and lavender baby soap that she'd washed him with earlier that afternoon. She'd been reluctant to put him down until Reuben had invited her to supper. She laid him gently into the cradle bed in the great room, then entered the kitchen as Reuben was closing the refrigerator door. He hadn't taken out any food. Had he changed his mind about her staying? "Reuben?"

He gave her a rueful smile. "I should clean up first before we have supper. It won't take long."

She eyed him, noting his damp shirt, his dusty pants and the blond hair that was plastered to his forehead. No man had ever looked better to her. *Ach nay*, she thought, *I'm in serious trouble*.

"I'll set the table," she said quietly.

He stared at her with an unreadable expression, before he nodded, then headed upstairs. She heard his heavy treads on the steps to the second floor, then the sound of water through the pipes.

She set the table and put out the cold fried chicken with the side dishes she'd made. Ellie had finished pouring two glasses of iced tea when she felt Reuben's presence. Detecting the scent of soap and clean male, she inhaled deeply, then faced him. Her heart beat hard at the sight of him. He wore a light green shirt with navy trousers. His hair was damp, and his feet were bare. "Do you feel better?" she asked politely.

"*Ja.*" His smile made her stomach flutter. His gaze went to the table. "Dinner looks delicious."

"I didn't heat the chicken. Do you want it warm? It won't take long."

"I like cold chicken."

"Me, too." She fiddled with the silverware, then put them beside their plates. Ellie felt awkward, nervous. She should be home with her parents, not eating with Reuben. She swallowed hard and turned. "I should get home."

He frowned. "You're not going to eat first?"

She shook her head. "I know I said that Charlie's there to help. But then I remembered she was with Nate this afternoon. What if she isn't home yet? I don't want Mam to worry about making dinner on her own. If I leave now I can still be a help to her."

"I see." He approached and she detected the heat, the clean scent, of him. "*Danki* for taking care of Ethan.

I shouldn't need your help for much longer." If he was disappointed that she was leaving, he didn't show it.

Ellie stiffened at the reminder that he wanted to get rid of her. "I forgot to tell you. I heard from Sarah today. It will be several more weeks before she can return." Giving him her back, she felt a headache coming on and absently lifted fingers to rub her forehead. "Until then, Charlie and I can take turns with Ethan."

Reuben was silent. As she faced him, she caught a strange look on his face. "Reuben?"

"I don't want to put you to any more trouble."

"Your son is no trouble," she said, meaning it.

He gazed at her. Whatever he read in her expression must have satisfied him. He finally nodded with a small smile. "How are you getting home?" he asked.

Ellie was startled. "I forgot! Charlie was supposed to come for me." She picked up her cell phone from the counter. "I'll call Nell." She felt his gaze on her as she dialed her sister. Once she explained to Nell what she needed, she hung up and turned to him. "My brother-in-law is close. He'll bring me home."

Reuben studied her without a word.

"Reuben?"

He shifted his attention to the table, where he sat and took a serving of macaroni salad, green beans and two pieces of the chicken.

She felt her stomach tighten as she watched him eat. Why wouldn't he talk to her? She could have—should have—stayed for supper, but it was too late now. James was already on his way.

Ellie checked on Ethan in the other room, then returned to find Reuben still eating. The tension between her and Reuben had become unbearable. She crossed the kitchen and exited out the side door. She'd rather wait in the yard for James than endure another moment inside.

She stood in the warmth of the early evening sun, but hugged herself with her arms. The chill deep inside wasn't physical.

She'd never been so glad when James pulled his wagon up to the house. She grinned at her brother-in-law. "I appreciate the ride."

"Charlie forgot, I take it," he said with an amused smile. "Too busy with her sweetheart?"

Ellie grinned again. "It would seem so."

He jumped down from the wagon and assisted her up before he returned to climb onto the driver's side.

As James steered the horse toward the road, she glanced at the house and froze. Reuben stood in the doorway with a strange expression on his face. He looked…anguished. She inhaled sharply and faced the front. Had she hurt him by leaving?

Nay. She was imagining things. Reuben wasn't upset.

She glanced back one last time and saw that Reuben had stepped outside to watch her leave. She didn't know what to think. The man confused her on many levels.

Should she return the next day? She would. For Ethan.

"How was your day?" James asked.

You don't want to know. "It was fine. How about yours?"

And she listened with interest as he told her about the vet visits he'd made that day and the problems he'd encountered with the animals. She made all the correct responses, despite that Reuben Miller was foremost in her mind.

Chapter Seven

The rest of the week went smoothly. Charlie watched Ethan in the morning while Ellie relieved her after work in the afternoon. Despite Ellie's concerns, her young charge seemed fine the day after she'd had trouble putting him to sleep. Ethan was in high spirits, giggling easily when she made faces or tickled him under the chin. His belly laugh was infectious. She burst out laughing each time he giggled whenever he decided something was funny.

Of Reuben, she'd seen very little. He left each morning after Charlie's arrival. When he came home in the afternoon, he was polite and infrequent with his smiles. Yet he behaved like a different person with her sister. He thanked her every morning for babysitting. When Ellie greeted him, he gave her a quiet nod, then traipsed upstairs for a shower. When he came down, she had supper on the table for him. Although she was annoyed with him, she'd continued to prepare it for him. It couldn't be easy for him to raise his child alone.

Her garden at home was doing well. This particular morning Ellie picked a number of vegetables, stored them in her buggy and brought them in with her when she relieved Charlie. During the last few days, she'd fixed a variety of meals for him with beef, ham and chicken. She guessed he liked her cooking because he always finished what she'd made him. Yet he'd never said a word.

At first she was upset with his reticence, but today she decided that she no longer cared. Better that there was silence between them than the exchanging of harsh words. Yet his stern, contemplative manner bothered her despite her decision not to care. She couldn't change the man. What he thought about her in his home with his son shouldn't matter. But for her, it did.

Surely he trusted her a little, or he wouldn't leave the house each morning knowing Ethan would be in her care every afternoon when he got home.

Ellie wondered why she bothered coming or cooking for him. And then she knew. She was trying to live like the Lord wanted her to. Feeling blessed, she wanted to help someone in need. And if that person—man—didn't want her help? It didn't matter. He needed her help if only temporarily, and that was good enough.

This afternoon she fixed a green bean and ham casserole, a dish easy to keep warm in the oven. The temperature and humidity, although it was summer, had eased off a bit, and there was a soft breeze sweeping the countryside. Ellie had opened the windows earlier to let in the fresh air.

Ethan played on the floor with a pot and the wooden spoon he loved. Ellie smiled down at him before she turned back to the stove to check on the simmering green beans she'd picked from her garden. Next, she took a ham steak from the refrigerator and cut it into small pieces to add to the green beans, along with dumplings she had yet to make. She'd bought the ham on the way after housecleaning for the Brodericks.

Thinking of Olivia Broderick made her feel sad—and blessed. The woman was undergoing cancer treatments, and she looked terrible. In such a short time, she'd lost weight and there were deep, dark circles under her eyes. Ellie had taken extra care this morning to ensure that the house was spic and span. Then she'd offered to make Olivia lunch. The woman had declined since she felt too nauseous to eat, but she'd thanked her with a smile, then handed her a wad of cash that was way more than Ellie normally charged. Olivia had been surprised when Ellie had insisted on giving her back the excess. Ellie had simply smiled and told her she'd be back in two weeks unless she needed her sooner. Olivia said she would call if she needed her before then. Ellie had left and stopped at the grocery store on her way. She'd bought not only the ham steak but also a beef roast and the ingredients for a number of easy casseroles. And last but not least, she'd purchased the ingredients for a chocolate cream pie.

Ethan napped peacefully for just over two hours before waking in good spirits. Ellie wished it was safe enough for her to take him outside to play, as the day was beautiful. But she couldn't, not as long as there was rusted metal and other junk in the yard. Instead, she gave him loving attention as she played with him on the floor in the great room where the floor was in better shape than in the kitchen.

The afternoon flew by. The next thing she knew, someone was entering the house. Picking up Ethan, she went out to greet Reuben after he turned from hanging his hat on a wall peg.

"*Hallo*, did you have a *gut* day?" she asked pleasantly.

He faced her, one eye clear but the other eye bloodshot and bright red.

"Reuben!" she exclaimed, hurrying toward him. "What happened?"

"Got a fragment of siding material in my eye." He regarded her carefully. "The doctor in the emergency room took out the sliver, but I have to put ointment in it for the next couple of days."

Feeling relief that he was okay, she nodded. "Would you like me to put some in for you?"

He didn't say anything at first, and she grew uncomfortable with her offer. He looked at her, then his son, before he returned his attention to her.

Taking his silence as a possible yes, Ellie went into the gathering room, picked the quilt off the floor and returned to the kitchen, where she laid it before she set Ethan down. The little boy cried out and held up his arms. She glanced at Reuben to find his blue gaze intent on her face. She gave Ethan the wooden spoon. "It won't take but a moment," she assured him, happy when Ethan finally settled down with his favorite toy. She held out her hand for the prescription ointment tube.

He gave it to her, then sat down and tilted his head back. Ellie stepped in close and was immediately aware of him as a man. His rugged scent. The warmth of his skin. The sound of his breathing. Her heart fluttered inside her chest as she unscrewed the cap. She felt the hitch in her breath as they locked gazes.

"Do you want to hold your eye open?" she asked.

"I trust you to do it."

She nodded, then reached for his bottom eyelid. She gently tugged downward and clicked her tongue in sympathy at the bright red that should have been the white of his eye. Ellie gently, capably squeezed out a single long bead across the bottom of his eye. She felt overwhelmed by being this close to him. "Blink several times," she instructed.

She stepped back, heart racing, as she concentrated on putting the cap back on the tube.

She sensed when Reuben straightened in the chair. She looked over and saw him blinking his eyes repeatedly. "Did I hurt you?" she asked softly. The last thing she wanted to do was cause harm to this man.

"Nay." He smiled at her. It had been so long since she'd seen his smile. The view was like a kick to her solar plexus. *"Danki."*

"You're *willkomm*." She reached for Ethan, who'd been watching Reuben and her together. She smiled as she lifted the boy into her arms. "Want to give a proper *hallo* to your *dat*?"

As if he understood, Ethan turned in her hold and reached for his father. Reuben stood and tugged him into his arms. He hugged Ethan and rubbed between his shoulder blades before returning his attention to Ellie.

"Danki," he said quietly. "For everything."

She was floored by his thanks. Was this goodbye? Was he telling her that he no longer needed her?

He frowned. "You don't have to come if it inconveniences you."

His worried expression eased her mind. It would have bothered her if this had been the end of her time with Ethan. *And Reuben.* "I don't mind watching Ethan.

He's such a sweet boy who is easy to love." She gasped, shocked by her words, which revealed too much to the child's father.

She was startled to see only relief in his expression. "I'll see you tomorrow." She grabbed her cloth shopping bag that she'd used to carry in the groceries. "There's supper in the oven. 'Tis just green bean and ham casserole." She hesitated. "I made chocolate cream pie for dessert." She inhaled sharply as a thought occurred to her. "I hope you like chocolate…"

He smiled. "I do."

She released a calming breath. "*Gut.* Have a nice night, Reuben." She reached out to stroke Ethan's sweet baby cheeks. "Behave for your *vadder*, little one."

Then she left with a last look at the house. To her surprise and pleasure, Reuben had stepped outside with his son. He didn't look stern or angry. His expression was soft, friendly. Ellie drew in a shaky breath and continued on, for she found this man hard to resist. And resist him she must because he would marry without love in order to give his son a mother. When she married one day, it would be to someone who offered her more.

Sunday was here before Ellie knew it. She hadn't seen much of Reuben in the last two days. He'd asked Charlie to stay with Ethan for the whole day yesterday, and Ellie couldn't help but feel hurt that he hadn't been happy with the arrangement she and her sister had worked out.

Ellie put on her best Sunday dress—a royal blue tab dress with white apron. She had washed and dried her hair the day before. After pinning her hair in place, she donned a black prayer *kapp*. She turned as Charlie entered the room.

"Mam and Dat ready?" she asked.

Charlie nodded. "*Ja*, they asked me to check on you."

"I'll be right down."

Her sister lingered. "I wonder if Reuben and Ethan will be at church," she said, startling Ellie.

"They haven't come yet."

"'Tis been difficult for him, I think." Her sister smiled. "He's settling in now. He worked with Jed again the other day."

Ellie blinked. "He did?"

"*Ja.* I saw Jed yesterday when he was at the house helping Nate." Charlie's gaze went soft at the mention of her betrothed, Nathaniel Peachy. "Reuben's been working on Jed's crew, but he'll be back managing his own construction site tomorrow."

"Reuben is foreman?"

"I got that impression."

She headed toward the door and her sister followed. "How's the *haus*?"

"'Tis *wunderbor*! I love it. I can't wait to wed and move in with Nate."

"You're eager for the *haus*? Or for Nate to be your husband?" She glanced at her sister, then grinned when Charlie blushed.

"I'm eager to marry Nate." Her cheeks remained a bright red. "I love him."

Ellie placed a hand on her youngest sister's shoulder. "I know you do, Charlie. Nate loves you, too."

Charlie's features lit up with happiness. Ellie longed to feel as Charlie did with Nate, but she would have to wait for some unknown future date. Helping her parents had to take precedence over finding a loving husband.

She descended the stairs with Charlie to join their parents. Mam smiled at them while she handed them each a cake to carry. Her mother held a large bowl of potato salad. All the dishes they brought would be shared at the midday meal after church service. The Peachys were hosting today, a fact that clearly thrilled her sister. Charlie looked excited, eager to see her betrothed, as Dat pulled their buggy onto the Abram Peachy farm. After her father parked the vehicle at the end of a long row of other buggies and wagons, Charlie jumped out with cake in hand and raced into the yard to look for Nate.

Ellie exited the vehicle more slowly. After laying the cake on the backseat, she helped her mother from the vehicle, then waited patiently for her father to join them. Ellie grabbed the cake, then accompanied her parents to the Peachy barn. The building was only a few years old, having been replaced after a fire caused by lightning. It was a nice structure with plenty of room for the congregation. In the summer months, members of their community often used barns for service. After a peek inside, Ellie took the salad bowl from her mother and headed to the house to set the cake and potato salad in the kitchen with the rest of the community's other food offerings.

It was as she was leaving the Abram Peachy farmhouse that she spied Reuben with Ethan. They must have just arrived, or she would have noticed sooner. She was surprised yet pleased to see them. She'd prayed and hoped that he'd feel comfortable attending church in his new community one day. Now that he was here, she realized he was finally settling in.

Charlie and Nate chatted with him. Her sister held out her arms and Ethan appeared happy to go to her. She eyed father and son with longing. How would it feel to have this man's attention and love? To have Ethan as a son?

She brought herself up short. *Dangerous thinking, Ellie.* She pretended she hadn't seen him as she crossed the yard to the barn. She nearly made it to the barn door when Charlie raced to join her with Ethan in her arms. The little boy took one look at Ellie and held out his arms. She shouldn't be glad that he wanted her, but she couldn't help it. He was a baby, only eight and a half months old. And he gave her such joy just to be near him.

"Service is about to begin," Nate murmured, having approached from behind.

Charlie smiled at him over her shoulder. "I'll see you after church."

Nate eyed her sister with softness that tugged at Ellie's heart.

They entered the dark interior of the barn. Once their eyes adjusted to the light, the room didn't seem dark at all. Ellie led the way, still holding Ethan, into the women's section, where she saw her sisters Leah and Nell. Meg was out of town. She and her husband, Peter, had gone for an extended visit to see Peter's grandparents in New Wilmington. She smiled at her sisters as she slid onto the same bench. Leah had grown larger with her pregnancy. There was happiness and contentment on her face that hadn't been visible before she'd married Henry Yoder.

Ellie was happy for her sisters. Each one of them had found a good man. Now their love was expanding to include children. Nell had learned she was two months pregnant only recently. She constantly smiled and glanced with love at James, her veterinary English-turned-Amish husband. James beamed back at her, clearly loving his wife and his life.

Ellie made sure Ethan was comfortable. If the boy had been older, he would have sat with his father in the men's section, but he was just a baby who needed his mother. Though a female friend would have to do since his mother was dead. Ellie felt a moment's heartbreak for the woman who never got to know her own child. She offered up a silent prayer for the woman and her family. Reuben was still grieving. It had to be hard for him to see his little boy resemble his wife, the woman he'd lost.

Church started and Ellie was amazed how well behaved Ethan was. Service took most of the morning. After singing and sermons that ran for hours, the congregation dispersed and headed outside. Ellie was exiting the barn with Ethan when Reuben approached.

"I'll take him," he said easily.

She nodded. She had work to do. She would help to put out the food. Without meeting his gaze, Ellie handed him Ethan, then went to the house to join the other women in the kitchen.

"Who's the little boy?" Alta Hershberger asked.

Ellie stiffened. Alta, the community busybody, didn't need to know the circumstances of her relationship with Ethan or Reuben. "He belongs to Reuben Miller. He moved into the community with his son and his sister."

Alta frowned. "His sister? I haven't seen the girl."

She sighed. She didn't want to natter, but Alta would be relentless if she didn't. She tempered her words as she explained. "Sarah is with her parents in Ohio. She's due back soon."

"Who's been watching the boy while she's gone?"

"My sister and I."

The woman narrowed her gaze. Ellie kept her expression light and smiling until Alta was forced to nod and return her smile. "That's kind of you."

Ellie shrugged. She was eager to escape the woman. Thankfully, Alta had decided she'd heard enough and left to natter to anyone who would listen. Ellie exhaled sharply and sent up a silent prayer of thanks that Meg wasn't here to complicate the situation.

Once the food was put out, she joined her family as they filled their plates. Ellie couldn't help her glance toward Reuben to see how he was doing. There were a number of young women around him apparently eager to help him and his baby boy. The sight of Reuben surrounded upset her. Did he envision one of the women as his future wife? She took her measure of the situation but received no clue to his thoughts. The few times she'd caught him smiling at a woman, even laughing once as he conversed with two of them, made her chest hurt. Apparently, it was just her he had a problem with. Especially since she knew he got along well with Charlie.

Her gaze shifted to Charlie and Nate, who had eyes only for each other. The start of their relationship hadn't been easy. At first, Nate had decided that he was too old for her sister, but thankfully time and Charlie had changed his mind.

With a small smile, Ellie poured herself some lemonade, then took a seat next to Nell.

"How is the cleaning business?" Nell asked.

"*Gut*. Got plenty of work to keep me busy. I'm glad I've cut back to a half a day, though."

Her sister nodded. "It can't be easy working for Englishers."

Ellie recalled one particular woman she had no desire to clean for again. Mara Golden had treated her like a servant, expecting her to pick up after her family before she cleaned house. She'd been condescending and cruel. Ellie had quickly suggested that she find someone else to clean for her. Mara hadn't taken the news well, but there had been nothing she could do or say that would have changed Ellie's mind.

The afternoon lengthened quickly. Ellie tried not to look at Reuben but found it impossible to avoid him. On one occasion, he locked gazes with her and she felt her chest tighten while her belly filled with butterflies. When Ethan fell asleep in his father's arms, she wanted to rush over to take the little boy and hold him close. Watching the two of them together made her feel warm inside.

Reuben stood with Ethan still sleeping against his shoulder. She saw him speak briefly with the people nearest to him before he headed toward the lot where everyone had parked their buggies.

He's leaving! Unable to resist, Ellie followed him. "Reuben," she called as she caught up to him.

He halted and turned. And his eyes became shuttered. "Elizabeth."

Ellie blinked and tried not to feel hurt by his reaction. "Do you still want Charlie and me to come tomorrow?"

"I don't want to put you to the trouble," he began.

"'Tis no trouble. I enjoy spending time with Ethan,

and so does Charlie." She managed a smile. "And 'tis better to have the same people watching him until your sister's return," she added.

She watched as the tension left his shoulders. "I'll see you tomorrow, then."

Ellie nodded. "Have a *gut* night," she said softly. "If you need us before…"

His lips quirked. "Call you?" he teased. "Not all of us own a cell phone."

She blushed. "*Ja.* Do you want one of us to stop by? To check if you need anything?"

"We'll be fine. Ethan's had a long day. I'm sure he'll fall right asleep."

"I'll see you tomorrow, then," she said as she turned. She started back toward the gathering.

"Ellie," he said, and she stopped, faced him. His expression was soft. "You are a *gut* friend."

Friend. Her smile hurt her cheeks as his face became shuttered. Feeling embarrassed that she'd sought him out, she rejoined her family in the Peachy backyard.

His thoughts were on Ellie as he put Ethan to bed, and remained on her throughout the night when he couldn't sleep. By Monday morning, he'd found a way to harden himself against her. The last thing he wanted was to fall for the young woman. And his guilt stabbed deep that he'd thought of her at all when his wife hadn't been dead a full year.

His son still slept as Reuben climbed out of bed and dressed. Forcing Ellie from his mind, he went into the kitchen for breakfast. He opened the refrigerator and froze. Besides leftovers, there were several days' suppers that Ellie had made for him. He chose the leftover egg casserole, then heated it up in a pan coated first with melted butter. Once it was hot, he sat down to eat, and the delicious taste brought his thoughts back around to Ellie. She'd make someone a good wife. She deserved someone who would love her. *Not someone like me*.

He finished eating just in time, as he heard his son's cry from upstairs. Reuben rose, put his dishes in the sink, then headed to fetch Ethan. Less than an hour later, Charlie arrived.

"*Gut* morning," she said with a smile. Her gaze warmed as it settled on Ethan. She held out her arms and the boy reached for her.

Reuben relinquished his hold, satisfied to see Ethan content in Charlie's arms. Once again, he thought of Ellie and the way Ethan had laid his head trustingly on her shoulder. The way she cuddled and rubbed his son's neck and back. His lips firmed. Why did it seem right for Ellie to hold him and not Charlie?

"Do you have everything you need?" he asked.

"*Ja,*" Charlie said. "I brought puffed wheat for Ethan."

He was quiet as he collected the lunch made from bread Ellie had baked and jelly she'd made fresh during strawberry season. He reached for his hat, then faced her. "Is Ellie coming to relieve you this afternoon?"

"She'll be here after she finishes work." She didn't meet his gaze as she answered. She was grinning at Ethan as she jostled him in her arms. His son's sudden laughter filled the room, making him smile.

"I'll be heading off," he said. She faced him then. "*Danki*, Charlie. I don't know how I would have managed with Sarah gone."

"'Tis our pleasure, Reuben. Ellie and I love children."

Ellie loves children. His heart thumped hard. "I'll see you tomorrow."

She nodded. "Have a *gut* day."

"The same to you," he said. As he steered his horse-drawn vehicle to Jedidiah Lapp's house, where he was to meet the construction crew, Reuben couldn't banish the mental image of a certain golden-blond-haired woman. Elizabeth Stoltzfus. She would continue to be a source of anxiety for him until he found a wife and married. Only then would he be able to move on with the future he envisioned for himself and Ethan, one with an uncomplicated wife, without the difficult feelings of loving someone.

Chapter Eight

"Ellie." Charlie stepped into the bedroom and regarded her sister. "I can't watch Ethan today."

Ellie turned from the window where she'd been fixing her hair as she'd admired the view outside. "I'll reschedule work," she said easily. She'd rather spend the day with the boy anyway. "Better yet, I'll call Rebecca Yoder to cover for me." And maybe she'd think about finding someone to take over her business for a while. Sarah still wouldn't be back for another few weeks yet.

"Are you sure?" Her sister appeared concerned.

"I'm certain." She smiled.

Charlie looked relieved. *"Gut. Danki."*

Ellie regarded her with surprise. "What are you thanking me for? You're the one helping me."

Her sister grinned. *"Ja.* I forgot about that."

After she left the room, Ellie dialed Rebecca, who, she knew, wouldn't mind taking over her work for the day. After she had Rebecca's consent, she called her two clients to inform them of the change. The first one was livid until she explained that her fill-in for the day was also Amish. The second one had no problems at all with the change.

She smirked. Why did Englishers think that Amish women were better at cleaning house?

Ellie glanced at her wristwatch and gasped. She needed to get to Reuben's before she was late. She grabbed the pie she'd baked for him from the refrigerator, then climbed into her pony cart and headed out.

She arrived five minutes later. She was early but not by much. Charlie was usually fifteen minutes early. As she headed toward the house, Reuben swung open the door, looking worried.

"I thought no one was coming," he said brusquely. He looked wonderful in a maroon shirt, black suspenders and navy tri-blend pants. She could see the muscles of his arms beneath his short shirtsleeves.

"I'm sorry. Charlie couldn't make it. I had to make a few phone calls before I came."

"If 'tis too much trouble…" he began.

"Nay." She tried to smile, but Reuben wasn't welcoming. Obviously, he preferred Charlie.

His eyes dropped down to the pie she held.

"Dried apple pie. I baked it last night. I hope you like dried apples."

His expression thawed. "I do."

She brushed past him and into the house. Ethan was in the high chair, and she immediately went to him. She caressed the top of his head, then bent to kiss it. The child looked up and smiled.

Reuben was silent. She could feel his gaze and spun. "Don't you have to work?"

He glanced at the wall clock and grimaced. *"Ja*, I need to go."

"You don't have to worry, Reuben. I'll take *gut* care of him."

"I never doubted that for a second," he replied sincerely. He grabbed his lunch bag from the counter.

"I'll see you when you get home," she said easily as he reached for his hat.

He stiffened. "You'll be spending all day with him?"

"*Ja*. Charlie is busy." She lifted her chin.

"Don't you have to clean house?"

"I made other arrangements."

He stared at her hard before he finally nodded. Then he left with mumbled words about being home at four this afternoon. Ellie watched him leave through the side kitchen window. Her heart was heavy as she realized that Reuben had hoped to see Charlie and not her.

She returned to Ethan, ensuring he had enough to eat. Today she'd teach him to drink from a cup, she decided. He was too old for a bottle. Ethan ate dry cereal by himself. Surely, he could learn to use a cup.

Ellie went to a cabinet to search for a cup for him. All she found were several glass tumblers and a small tin cup that she realized was a measuring cup.

"You and I will be going to the store today," she told Ethan with a smile. "I'm going to buy you a sippy cup."

Ethan kept eating, not understanding her or concerned with her decision to leave the house. While at the store, she'd also purchase a few groceries.

After breakfast, Ellie changed Ethan's diaper. She wished she'd brought the buggy. It would have been safer for Ethan to ride in. She called Nell on her cell. Nell was allowed a phone because of her husband's veterinary practice.

"Can we switch vehicles for the day?" she asked, explaining why.

"I can pick up what you need," Nell said. "I'm in Whittier's Store."

Ellie gave her a list over the phone.

"I'll be there as soon as I can," Nell promised.

After thanking her sister, Ellie hung up the phone and smiled at Ethan. "Wouldn't you like to be outside and enjoy this delightful summer breeze?" she asked softly. The boy laughed and she grinned. "What's so funny, little man?"

After she cleaned him up, she grabbed a quilt and took Ethan outside to play just outside the side door. On impulse, she brought the pot and spoon he loved. The summer breeze was pleasant. It had rained during the night, and the temperature had cooled down to the upper seventies.

Ethan loved being outside. He sat on the quilt, banging on the pot with the spoon. Watching him, Ellie got an idea. She stood and reached down for him. He looked at her and his lips quivered. "*Nay*, sweetheart, we're not going inside."

He appeared on the verge of tears, and she hugged him close. The sudden stark realization that she was here with Ethan when his young mother was cold in the ground made her feel sorry for Susanna. For Reuben, who had lost the woman he loved.

She closed her eyes as she held Ethan tight. The boy struggled in her arms, clearly wanting to get down. She crouched, set him on his feet, then, holding on to his hands, she kept him upright and urged him to take a few steps. Ellie took joy as Ethan tried, putting one foot in front of the other. He would have fallen if she'd let go, but she kept a close, loving eye on him as she held on to him. When she sensed he'd grown tired of the game, she set him down, then handed him his spoon and pot. She watched with a smile as he went back to hitting the bottom of the pot with the spoon handle.

A while later Ellie could tell Ethan was tired. Glancing at her watch, she was startled by the hour. "Lunch, Ethan, and then nap time."

She fed him cooked mashed carrots for lunch, which he clearly enjoyed, as he ate every bite. She then gave him a handful of Cheerios. Ethan devoured them, then leaned back in the high chair with heavy-lidded eyes. "Time for a nap," she said.

Ellie put Ethan in the bed in the next room. The child turned on his side and promptly fell asleep. With a smile, she returned to the kitchen, made herself a sandwich, then cleaned up.

Nell arrived and handed her the requested items. Ellie paid her, then waved as her sister left to join her husband at a nearby farm.

Knowing that Ethan would sleep for an hour and a half, at least, Ellie put away the groceries and set the blue-and-white child's sippy cup on the kitchen counter. Next, she took out a broom and swept the kitchen floor. Should she cook the beef roast? The day was cool enough for the oven. The breeze wafting through the open windows would help modulate the indoor temperature. Ellie then wiped down the countertops before she headed upstairs to collect dirty laundry. As she carried the clothes basket downstairs, she experienced the strangest feeling. Doing Reuben's laundry felt like something only a wife would do. But Sarah had done the wash, she thought. And so could she.

She frowned as she filled the washer with colored clothes.

Would Sarah call today? She hoped so. Maybe she should call and leave a message for the girl. It would be good to talk with her, to ask after Reuben's mother. Yet she hesitated about calling. If Sarah was returning, then Reuben would no longer need her.

She froze. The thought of leaving shouldn't bother her, but it did.

The downstairs chores complete, Ellie made a cup of tea, then sat at the kitchen table and sipped from it. She didn't want to think about the time she would no longer get to see Reuben daily. She didn't want to think about leaving Ethan, the sweet child who'd captured her heart.

She took a swallow of tea, then paused. She thought she heard the sound of running water. She didn't think much of it at first, believing it to be the washer in the back room. But then she heard the washer spin and realized that the steady sound of water flowing had continued when it should have stopped. She got up and went to check on the washing machine. The machine had stopped, yet the sound of water continued—and it wasn't coming from this room.

With a frown, she headed toward the stairs and paused at the bottom, where the sound of water was louder. She raced up the steps and found the source. Water sprayed from under the sink and flooded the floor. Heart racing, Ellie wondered how to turn off the main water line. The leak appeared to be from the other side of the sink's turnoff valves. She ran downstairs and found the main valve in the mudroom where the washer and drier were located. She turned it and was relieved when the sound halted.

Ellie hurried to check on Ethan, who stirred as he woke up. She gasped. Water had leaked through the great room ceiling not far from where Ethan had slept. *We can't stay here.*

She'd take Ethan home with her. They couldn't stay here without water. She'd make sure they were back before Reuben was expected home.

She would try to reach him first so he wouldn't worry. She dialed the construction company, but the call wouldn't go through. She waited a few minutes, then tried again.

She called her sister Leah at her store, Yoder's Craft Shop and General Store. Her sister and her husband, Henry, had recently started carrying groceries again. The shop had been a general store until Henry's parents had turned it over to Leah for a craft shop. Henry, a cabinetmaker, kept furniture items as well as sample kitchen and bath cabinets in the store, as well.

"Yoder's Craft and General Store," her sister announced as she answered the phone.

"Is Henry there?"

"Ellie! He's up at the house."

Ellie bit her lip. "Do you think he would mind trading vehicles with me? I'm watching Reuben Miller's son, and there's been a water pipe leak. I had to shut off the main water valve, and I'd like to take Ethan to Mam and Dat's, but I have the pony cart."

Leah chuckled. "I'll send Henry over with a buggy seat," she said.

"A buggy seat?"

"Just something Henry made with our future son or daughter in mind."

"And it will hold an eight-month-old?"

"Ja."

"Danki."

"I'll call up to the house and tell him."

"I appreciate it."

"I'll expect you to watch your niece or nephew when needed."

Ellie grinned. "It would be my pleasure." She loved children. She had yet to watch Meg's baby, and now with her two other older sisters pregnant, there would be more little ones to love.

Henry arrived twenty minutes later. He grinned as he saw her in the yard with Ethan. "Special delivery," he said.

She gave him a wide smile. "I'm happy to see you and your thing—whatever it is."

He took out a wooden seat, which he strapped onto the pony cart seat beside her. It was the perfect size for a child. Once it was in place, he met her gaze. "All set. He'll be safe in this."

"Danki."

"You're *willkomm*."

"How is Leah feeling?"

He beamed at her. *"Wunderbor."*

"You'll be a *gut vadder*."

"I hope so."

"No doubt about it." She shifted Ethan in her arms. "I should go. I want to get to Mam and Dat's and back before Reuben gets home. You know they're going to want one of these."

Henry grinned. "I'll be glad to make them one." He helped her onto her cart. "I'll see you on Sunday."

Ellie nodded, then watched him get into his own vehicle and leave. Minutes later, she arrived home. Her parents were surprised but happy to see her and Ethan.

"What's wrong?" her father asked.

Ellie explained the situation.

He listened carefully, then asked for the house key. "We'll get it fixed up for you."

She gave him the key, and he immediately left to get his brother-in-law, her uncle Samuel, to see if they could fix the leak.

Dat and Uncle Samuel returned an hour later. "We were able to fix the leak," her father said.

"And you turned the water back on?"

"*Ja*, we had to check to make sure the repair held, and it did."

Ellie released a sharp breath. "I should get back, then. I tried to call where Reuben works but I haven't been able to get through. The phone lines must be down."

"We saw a car accident between here and the house," her uncle said. "Looks like the driver hit an electric pole."

"I hope no one was seriously hurt." She murmured a quick, silent prayer that the driver and any passengers were well.

"There was an ambulance on the scene. I don't know how many were in the car."

Ellie nodded. "I'll be careful going back. Should I take a different road?"

Her father agreed that it would be best if she drove back via a different avenue. He told her which way to go. She nodded in agreement before she picked up Ethan, then left.

Despite the seat that kept Ethan safe, Ellie steered her vehicle slowly back to the Reuben Miller house. She left the pony cart in her parents' yard, opting to take the family buggy instead. The wooden seat that Henry made fit well in the buggy, and she was glad she'd called Leah to ask for help.

It took her a little longer to get back to the house since she was forced to take a different route. She was relieved when she caught sight of the house ahead. She'd approached from the opposite direction, and she turned on the directional signal and pulled into the yard. To her shock, she saw a buggy parked near the hitching post. Reuben was already home.

She pulled in next to his vehicle and closed her eyes briefly in preparation for the coming confrontation. The man wouldn't be happy to have her gone from the house with his son.

Breathing deeply to calm herself, Ellie got out, then skirted the buggy to take Ethan from his seat. When she turned, Reuben stood outside near the side door.

She approached. "Reuben."

"Where have you been?" he demanded harshly.

"With my parents."

"Why? Because you can't manage to stay a whole day?"

She brushed by him to enter the house. He followed her but she refused to answer him.

"Elizabeth!"

She spun to face him. "I'm not a child, Reuben."

"You left."

"I had a *gut* reason." She felt Ethan struggle within her arms. She could sense his upset, and she quickly soothed him with a gentle caress on his head and back.

Reuben eyed her skeptically. "What reason?" He

didn't look as fierce, but his expression hadn't softened either.

"You had a water leak. I had to shut off the water to the house. 'Tis hard to care for a child without water."

His blue eyes darkened. "Where?" His tone suggested that he didn't believe her.

"In the upstairs bathroom." She marched with Ethan into the gathering room and pointed toward the wet ceiling.

Reuben followed her. It was only after he saw what she meant that he frowned. He gave a heavy sigh. "I'll get my tools."

"No need," she said stiffly. "The leak is fixed. My father and uncle took care of it."

"What?" His tone was soft, as if he was trying to control anger.

"I said—"

"I know what you said," he cut in. "What right did you have to allow strangers into my home?"

"They're not strangers—"

"They're your family, not mine! You had no business inviting them into my *haus*. I could've fixed the leak."

She strapped Ethan into his high chair. "Reuben, they offered and I couldn't say *nay*," she said softly. "It took them less than an hour—and that with time to get here and back."

"The time it took is irrelevant. It's up to me to take care of my house. I don't need your interference."

"Why is it so hard for you to accept help, Reuben?" she cried. "I don't understand you at all. My father and Uncle Samuel were trying to help you. You have a lot on your mind. They thought they were doing a *gut* thing!"

"I can take care of my own!"

"Apparently." She sighed. "It's getting late. I should leave."

"Fine." His tone was sharp, the one word abrupt.

She released a cleansing breath, then turned to run a caring hand over Ethan's shoulder. "Take care, little man. I'll see you tomorrow."

"There's no need for you to come back tomorrow," Reuben said evenly, making her blanch.

Ellie nodded and left, wondering how a simple helpful gesture had gone so wrong.

She blinked back tears as she climbed into her buggy and headed home. She wouldn't tell her father about Reuben's reaction. Her *dat* had done a good thing, and no one was going to make him feel bad about it.

Hurt, she tried not to think of the near future. She would miss Ethan. More than she should, she realized. She had gotten too emotionally involved with him and his mercurial father. It was probably for the best that she didn't go back.

Yet a painful constriction in her chest told her differently. That she'd rather spend time with Ethan—and his father—than clean house. These last two weeks, she'd felt so alive.

Was this how Charlie felt when she was with Nate? And Leah with Henry? Nell with James? Meg with Peter?

She thought of her parents. They had a good marriage. She saw the subtle looks they exchanged, which suggested a solid relationship. A partnership. That was what she wanted with a husband some day. She sighed. Was that why Reuben was a bitter man? Because he'd lost that time, that partnership, with his young wife?

That night, as she climbed into bed, she decided that

it didn't matter if Reuben didn't want her to come. She would go anyway. The man and his son needed her, whether he liked it or not. With that decision made, she went to bed and slept well.

When she woke the next morning, she wondered if it was still a good idea—going to Reuben's as if he hadn't dismissed her the day before.

She was at the kitchen table eating breakfast when there was a knock at the back door. Ellie rose to answer it, her eyes widening as she saw Reuben with his son on her doorstep.

"Reuben?"

"I need to talk with you."

She stepped back and allowed him to enter.

Chapter Nine

"Ellie," he murmured as he stepped into the room. "Elizabeth."

She studied him carefully. "What's wrong?"

"I've been called in to work." Reuben looked sheepish, apologetic. "I can't take care of Ethan."

The man appeared anguished. She saw the pain in his blue eyes, the sorrow in his handsome features. "You want me to watch him?"

"I have no right to ask."

Ellie arched an eyebrow. "I don't have a problem with giving or accepting help, Reuben. You do."

He glanced away. "I know. I'm sorry."

She was stunned. "'Tis *oll recht*." She reached out for Ethan, and Reuben released his little son into her arms.

He wouldn't meet her gaze. She could feel the tension emanating off him, the confusion, his fear.

"I'll take *gut* care of him."

He nodded as he raised his eyes to lock gazes with her. *"Danki."*

"You should go before you're late."

"Ja." He shifted. "I would have come to apolo-

gize even if I hadn't been called to work. I was...ill-mannered and ungrateful."

"Your usual self," she quipped with good humor.

His features relaxed as a spark of amusement entered his blue eyes. "I've never met anyone like you," he said.

Ellie frowned, unsure if it were a good or bad thing that he thought her different. Vaguely, she wondered what he would have thought if she'd marched up to his house this morning, despite his unwillingness to have her in his home and with his child.

"I'm one of a kind," she finally agreed.

He smiled. "I'll stop after work to pick him up unless..."

"I'll be happy to take him home in a little while," she said. "As long as you don't mind me in your *haus* again."

Regret flickered in his gaze. "That would be fine."

Ellie was surprised when he hesitated before leaving. "Don't you have to get moving?"

Reuben blinked. "*Ja.* I will see you after work."

"*Ja*, you will."

Since she'd already called Rebecca to cover for her today, Ellie brought Ethan inside to have some breakfast before she took him back to the house. It must have taken a lot for Reuben to come and apologize. It said a lot for his character. He did it because he needed her, but still, it couldn't have been easy. She recalled the regret in his blue eyes. He felt bad about the way he'd treated her, though she found it easy to forgive him.

An hour later, Ellie and Ethan headed home. She used the key Reuben had given her to unlock the door. She stepped inside and took stock of her surroundings. The kitchen was sparkling clean. Had Reuben eaten?

There was no sign of dishes, either in the sink or drying in the drain rack.

Why am I worried about him? He wouldn't appreciate it.

The day went quickly. Ellie cleaned the rooms upstairs while Ethan napped downstairs. She stopped what she was doing often to check on him, but the little boy continued to sleep. Then she heard a sound at the side door announcing Reuben's arrival. She was on the great room floor changing Ethan's diaper when Reuben walked in. *"Hallo,"* he greeted pleasantly. He sounded friendly.

"Reuben, *hallo.* Did you have a *gut* day?"

He nodded. "We got a lot done."

"Gut," she murmured as she fastened Ethan's clean diaper. Holding him by the waist, she stood Ethan on his legs. The baby laughed with delight and reached out a hand toward her prayer *kapp.* She chuckled. *"Nay,* you don't, little man!"

She felt Reuben's intense regard and glanced at him. Ellie was surprised to see a soft expression on his face. She stood and held Ethan out to his father. "Would you mind?"

He took his son easily and without hesitation, holding him in one arm while he watched Ellie, who picked up the wet diaper to dispose of in the diaper pail to be washed later.

"Are you hungry?" she asked as she returned. "There are potatoes and sausages in the oven. I hope you like them."

He gazed at her a long time with what looked like awe. "I do. I haven't had them since I was a child."

Ellie beamed at him. "I hope these are as *gut* as those

you remember." She collected her bag, rubbed Ethan's back where he lay cuddled in his father's arms, then headed into the kitchen. "I'll see you tomorrow."

Reuben had followed her. "Don't you have to work?"

She shook her head. She had asked Rebecca to cover her workload for the entire week. Thankfully, Rebecca had agreed. She'd stop by Rebecca's house on the way home to confirm. "I'm available to watch him."

He nodded. "I'll see you tomorrow, then." He no longer appeared to mind her in his house, spending time with his son. She sighed with pleasure. Being friends with Reuben was better than being at odds with him.

As she steered her buggy home, she tried not to think about why it was wrong to cook for Reuben, care for his child and clean his house. She found she enjoyed babysitting better than cleaning Englishers' houses. And therein lay the problem. She was filling in for Reuben's sister until her return or until the man found himself a wife. A wife he wouldn't love. A woman he wanted only as a mother for Ethan.

For the next few days, Ellie went to Reuben's after her morning chores. It was more or less an amicable arrangement. The tension of those early days between them had dissipated. She and Reuben were friendly to each other, and the time flew by quickly until she realized with amazement that it was already Friday afternoon. As Ellie had thought, Charlie was happy to spend time with Nate before school started again and she would be back teaching in the classroom. Her sister came home each night with a goofy smile of love and affection for her man still on her face.

Reuben greeted her warmly at the end of each workday, and she felt something blossom inside. She wasn't sure what she was feeling, but it felt good. Tomorrow was Saturday, but he still wanted her to come. She would go after she did what she could to help her parents. And she'd make sure Charlie was available to help while she was absent.

The next morning, she rose early and went to take care of the animals, as usual. As she fed the goats, she was happy to see her sister enter the barn. "Charlie, did you sleep well?"

Charlie smiled. "Like a baby."

"Not a crying newborn, I hope," she teased.

Her sister laughed. *"Nay."*

"Charlie," Ellie said, her tone serious, "will you be home today?"

"Ja, why?"

"Reuben wants me to watch Ethan, but I want to make sure Mam and Dat have the help they need."

Charlie frowned, as if puzzled. "I'll be here. Nate may stop over later. He can help Dat if he needs anything."

Ellie felt the tension leave her frame. *"Danki."*

"You love that little boy, don't you?"

She nodded. "He's a sweet baby."

"And the father isn't ugly either," her sister teased.

"Reuben has nothing to do with this," she insisted.

Charlie narrowed her eyes but said nothing. She turned back to grooming one of the horses as Ellie went outside with a bucket of chicken feed.

When she was done with the animals, Ellie went to the house to collect her bag and the chocolate cake she'd baked for Reuben. As she took it off the washer in the back room, she wondered why she'd baked for him again. Her sister's words came back to jolt her. *And the father isn't ugly either.*

It was true. Reuben was an extremely handsome man and she was attracted to him. But she knew better than to think that anything could happen between them. Especially given his decision to marry not for love but for Ethan.

"I'm leaving, Mam," she called as she came out of the room. Her mother turned from the kitchen sink, where she'd been washing the breakfast dishes. "I should have helped you with those," she said apologetically.

"I can handle the dishes, Ellie," her mother replied with a smile.

Ellie noted that her *mam* looked well today. The dark circles that she'd seen under her mother's eyes were gone, as if a good night's sleep had erased them. "I feel like I haven't been around much to help out," she said softly.

"With what?" Missy Stoltzfus looked confused. "I manage fine without help."

"But Charlie will be home today, *ja*?"

Mam smiled. "*Ja*. And Nate. She loves that young man. 'Tis *gut* to see them together."

She nodded. "They are eager to be man and wife."

"I want the same happiness for you."

"Mam…"

"You work too hard. I think you like caring for Ethan Miller because you love children." Missy eyed her silently. "You'd make a *gut mudder* to Ethan."

"*Nay.* I'm just helping until Sarah comes back."

"You seem happier spending time with the child than you are cleaning *haus* for Englishers."

"Mudder…"

Her mother shrugged as she smiled. "Just a thought." She reached into a cabinet and pulled out a box of baby cookies. "Take these for Ethan. I'm sure he'll love them."

Ellie blinked, stunned that her mother had purchased something for Reuben's son. "Mam, I'm not marrying the man. Ethan will not become your grandchild."

Mam chuckled. "With God's blessing, one can always pray and hope."

His son was still sleeping after Reuben had been up well over an hour and a half. He needed to get work done on the house, but he didn't want to disturb Ethan's rest. A quick glance at the wall clock in the kitchen made him wonder what time Ellie planned to come. It was nearly eight thirty. Had they arranged a time? He frowned. He didn't think they had.

Once Ellie arrived, he'd ask her whether or not it would be wise to wake Ethan. He'd hoped to replace the flooring downstairs. He'd purchased linoleum for a reasonable sum, and would install the same pattern in the kitchen and great room. It was an unusual pattern for linoleum flooring. Made of heavy vinyl, it resembled wood. Linoleum was best kept clean with a damp mop, and a lot of Amish families used it in their houses.

He opened the side door to allow in air. The day looked promising. Not too hot or humid, with a light breeze wafting in from outside. He put the coffeepot on to perk, then went outside to sit in the morning sun. The sound of carriage wheels drew his attention as Ellie steered her pony cart toward the barn and parked. She hopped out, tied up her horse, then skirted the vehicle to head toward the house.

She froze, faltering, when she saw him. But then she approached with a smile on her face. "Reuben, *gut* mornin'. Have you had breakfast?"

He shook his head, noting how pretty she looked in a pink dress with black apron and white head covering. Her blond hair was neatly pulled back and tucked underneath her *kapp*. "Just put a pot of coffee on the stove."

"And Ethan?"

"Still sleeping." He studied her with a frown. "That's *oll recht, ja*? That he's still sleeping?"

She smiled in reassurance. "'Tis fine. He's a little boy who needs his rest. He had a busy day yesterday." She went to the counter and set down the chocolate cake she'd brought. "I made chocolate."

He grinned. "Sounds *gut*."

"Would you like eggs and bacon?" She reached into the refrigerator for the carton of eggs and package of bacon.

Reuben stared. He hadn't gone shopping lately. Were the eggs from when Sarah was here? He must have said something aloud, because Ellie answered.

"I brought a few things with me yesterday." She paused. "I hope you don't mind."

He opened his mouth, then closed it. To object would make him ungrateful. They were just eggs and bacon, after all. He watched her get out a frying pan, then add a pat of butter. The coffeepot had finished perking, and Ellie turned off the gas burner, then grabbed him a mug and poured him a cupful. She silently handed it to him, then turned her attention back to making his breakfast.

"Aren't you going to eat?" he asked when he saw she'd made enough for only one.

"*Nay*, I ate before I came."

"You don't have to cook for me, Ellie."

"I don't mind. I like cooking."

He felt himself smile. *"Oll recht. Danki."*

In a few short minutes, she had heated the pan, cooked his bacon and eggs and dished them onto a plate. He sat down at the table and was about to suggest that she sit with a cup of coffee when he heard his son cry out.

"I'll get him," Ellie said with a grin. "I'm sure the little man needs to be changed before he eats."

Reuben watched her leave, marveling at the easy way she had about her. She made him feel relaxed, content. It was only as he remembered Susanna and his decision to marry for Ethan rather than love that he stiffened his spine and hardened his heart.

When she came into the room a few minutes later with Ethan, he had the mind-set to ignore the fact that she was pretty. Or that he'd been attracted to her for a minute. *Or fifty.*

Ethan smiled, obviously happy to be up, as Ellie set him in the high chair.

"Would you like more coffee?" she asked.

He rose from the table. *"Nay*, I should get to work."

She took a box of cereal out of the pantry and dumped some onto Ethan's tray. "What are your plans for today?"

"I'd like to install flooring here and in the great room, but since you and Ethan are here…"

"I can take him home with me if you'd like."

He jumped at her offer. If he didn't, he was afraid he'd find himself thinking about how pretty she was again. "I'd appreciate that."

She blinked. "How long do you need us to be gone?"

"Until this afternoon? About three or so?"

Ellie nodded. "Come, little man. You can finish your breakfast at my *haus*."

Without meeting his gaze, Ellie packed a bag for Ethan, then reached for her purse. "Help yourself to the cake. I think there is still lunch meat if you'd like a sandwich later."

And then Ellie left, taking Ethan with her. The house suddenly seemed empty and silent. Too silent. The afternoon, when they would return, seemed a long way off. There was just one thing to do—get to work. He would start in the kitchen, then move into the great room. Once he laid the flooring, they would have to stay off it until the glue set well. And if he got it done soon, he could head over to the Arlin Stoltzfus household to invite Ellie and his son home. Maybe he could offer to buy her supper.

He scowled. What happened to keeping his mind-set about women and marriage?

Reuben released a huge sigh and went out to get the rolled linoleum he'd purchased a while ago out of the barn.

Ellie was disappointed and she didn't know why. She enjoyed taking care of Ethan. It had nothing to do with Reuben Miller. Or did it? It bothered her how quickly he'd accepted her offer of leaving with Ethan.

Her mother grinned as Ellie entered the house with the boy. "What a nice surprise!" She held out her arms and Ethan reached for her.

With a chuckle, Ellie relinquished her hold on the little boy. "He feels comfortable with you, Mam."

"He is a sweetheart."

Rebecca Kertz 127

She watched her mother hug and love on Reuben's child and wondered whether she'd been disappointed that she'd had five daughters and no sons. Ellie asked her.

Mam looked at her with frown. "*Nay.* I've never been disappointed. Neither has your *vadder.* You girls have given us great joy. You were sweet youngsters and have grown up to be fine young women."

Suddenly misty-eyed, Ellie gazed at her. "I love you, Mam."

Her mother regarded her with warmth. "I love you, *dochter.*"

"Ethan hasn't finished his breakfast."

"Let's make sure he has plenty to eat, then, shall we?" Mam ran a gentle finger along Ethan's baby-smooth cheek.

Ellie worked in the kitchen with her mother and Charlie while Ethan played on the kitchen floor. When it was time for lunch, the three women ate sandwiches and fixed a plate for Dat. Ellie held Ethan while she gave him some cooked carrots that had cooled off enough for him to pick up and eat. The little boy enjoyed them immensely, eagerly grabbing up another one, then shoving it into his mouth. For dessert, she gave him a cookie especially made for babies. Holding it with both hands, he chewed on it with a grin, then held it up for her inspection. Ellie smiled and praised him until she was sure he had eaten all that he wanted. She then cleaned him up and put him down for a short nap.

At three o'clock, she grabbed her market tote and Ethan's bag and put them in the backseat after settling Ethan in his buggy seat up front. She, her mother and Charlie had baked five loaves of bread and two butter pound cakes today. Her tote carried a loaf of bread and one cake for Reuben. As she steered the buggy toward his house, she eyed the passing scenery, glorying in the sunny afternoon. She wondered how Reuben had made out with the flooring.

The man was outside with a cold drink when she drove up to the hitching post. She got out, then reached in for Ethan, but left their bags in her vehicle. Straightening, she glanced toward the house and encountered Reuben's intense blue gaze.

Heart skittering in her chest, she approached and managed a smile. "Reuben," she greeted with a nod.

"Elizabeth."

She frowned. When he used her given name, she felt as if he was putting her in her place. What had she done wrong now? "Did you finish the floor?"

"*Ja*. We should be able to walk on it now." He smiled, and the change made her catch her breath. "Want to see?"

Filled with excitement, she followed him into the house. She stepped in the kitchen and halted. Her eyes widened. The floor looked beautiful—shiny wood that added to the appeal of the room. "You put this wood down in one afternoon?" she asked, astonished.

Pleased by her reaction, Reuben grinned. "'Tis not wood, El. 'Tis linoleum. Here. Feel." He felt the warmth of her skin as he took her hand, then pulled her down to touch the floor. Ethan squirmed in her arms.

Reuben reached for his son. "Come here, little man. Now you can sit and play on this new floor without a blanket." He set his son carefully in the middle of the kitchen and straightened.

"It looks lovely," Ellie murmured as she walked farther into the room. The soft, awed way she said it smacked him hard in his chest.

He reined in his feelings. Ellie Stoltzfus churned up something inside him he didn't want or need. "'Tis a floor," he said with less warmth.

She glanced at him, her blue eyes wide. "Is something wrong?"

Reuben felt immediately contrite. It wasn't as if she'd done anything to upset him. He had done that entirely on his own. "*Nay*, everything is fine." He managed a smile. "I appreciate you taking him with you this morning. I wasn't sure how I'd get all this done with him here."

Ellie nodded. "*Ja*, I can understand that." He sensed her sudden discomfort as she turned away. "I should get our bags in from the buggy."

Definitely uncomfortable, he thought. It was as if she was using an excuse to escape. He allowed her to leave, watching with pleasure as Ethan scooted across the floor on his hands and knees. *When did he start doing that?*

The thought came that he should pick Ethan up, then follow Ellie to help with the bags.

The door opened and Ellie entered with two bags, one he recognized as belonging to his son. The other one was hers. He'd seen it before. With a brief smile in his direction, she went to the table and set down both bags. She opened her bag and pulled out two wrapped loaves of bread and a large round plastic container. "I brought bread and cake." She picked up the bread loaves and set them on the counter close to the refrigerator. "Are you hungry? I can cut you a piece of cake."

"You brought me bread and cake," he muttered, floored. She was always doing something nice for him and Ethan. Was it any wonder that she'd been the focus of his thoughts a lot lately? She was a friend. A helpful friend, and while he didn't like taking help from anyone, he didn't mind that she was helping Ethan. He had simply benefited from her presence and care of Ethan.

She was eyeing him warily. "You don't want my bread and cake?" she asked quietly.

He made a quick decision. "I'll have a slice of each."

When she grinned, looking pleased, he knew he'd made the right choice. After all, he had to think of Ethan. If he upset his caretaker, then where would he be?

He simply ignored the niggling inside that suggested he was fooling himself to believe his only concern was Ethan.

Chapter Ten

Ellie returned, expecting to find Reuben busy working somewhere in the house or outside in the yard. Seeing him on the front porch, relaxing, made her stomach flip-flop and her breath hitch. He was so handsome, and she didn't want to notice. Worse yet, she liked him, and she couldn't afford to have feelings for him, for he only wanted a woman in his life who was uncomplicated, a mother for his child—and nothing else. She would watch Ethan until Sarah returned and then continue her life without them.

It was heartwarming to see Reuben enjoy the bread she'd made, sliced and buttered for him. She found more enjoyment from watching him eat her pound cake. When he was done, he stood and excused himself to work upstairs, and Ellie cleaned up the dishes, then fed Ethan dinner. She had picked up a few jars of baby food, although she preferred to mash vegetables that she'd grown and cooked herself. But she hadn't given it a thought until she was on her way over when she'd stopped at the store for a quick purchase of baby green beans, squash and turkey with vegetables…all smooth and easy foods for this little boy to eat.

After Ethan had eaten, she cleaned his face, then changed his clothes and his diaper. By then, it was getting near suppertime at home. She went to the bottom of the stairs and called up to Reuben that it was time she headed back.

He appeared seconds later at the top of the stairs. "'Tis that late?"

She nodded. "*Ja.* I fed Ethan and he's ready for bed whenever you're ready. Unless you want me to put him down now?" She waited a heartbeat.

"*Nay,*" he said. "I'll come down and spend some time with him. I can't do any more up here right now anyway." He came down the steps, and Ellie moved back as he reached the bottom stair. She could detect his scent. He had washed up earlier, and the lingering odor of soap and male that belonged only to Reuben reached her senses. She drew a sharp breath as she waited for him to precede her into the gathering room, where Ethan played on the floor with a wooden toy.

Reuben grinned when he saw Ethan, and Ellie noted the resemblance between father and son, which reached out to tug on her heartstrings.

"There is some leftover ham and lima beans with dumplings in the refrigerator for you for supper," she said. "So I'll be off." Ellie picked up her bag. "Will I see you tomorrow?" she asked. "'Tis visiting Sunday and my family is hosting. I hope you will come." Feeling herself blush, she turned. "Have a *gut* night, Reuben."

"Have a pleasant evening, Elizabeth. I'll see you tomorrow," he murmured behind her.

His soft tone drew her gaze to his face one more

time. His expression was warm, easy, and Ellie knew she was lost. *Ach nay!* She cared deeply for this man.

She left hurriedly to get home in time for supper. She'd helped her mother make sides for a roast beef dinner before she'd left to bring Ethan home. She forced her thoughts to the meal and spending time with her parents and her sister. But Reuben's attractive features and smile kept returning to her thoughts.

She swallowed hard. She should find someone to take over watching Ethan, but she couldn't bear not to spend time with him...and his father.

She thought of the day she'd had. She wouldn't have left if there had been some place for her and Ethan to go while Reuben installed the flooring. While it was good that she'd been at the house for her mother, today had been one of those times when she wasn't needed by her parents. Charlie was still in residence and she'd spent the entire day there, with Nate arriving just as Ellie left to take Ethan back to Reuben.

Ellie thought of the yard. If not for the rusted junk on the property, it would be a fine place to take Ethan outside to enjoy the warm balmy days of summer and the upcoming fall. An idea came to her while she parked her vehicle next to Nate Peachy's. She could enlist her family to clean up the yard while Reuben was at work on a construction site. He no longer worked with any of her cousins. He was foreman again on another job. A perfect opportunity to get the work done, as long as her cousins could afford to take the time. *I'll ask them. If they can't, they can't, but maybe they will be able to help him.*

She was afraid that Reuben wouldn't be open to the idea, but she would go ahead with her plans anyway.

Although he tried, the man couldn't handle everything on his own. He was only one person, and he had a full community of workers at his disposal. But she would ask only her family. And pray that he wouldn't be too angry once he realized what she'd done.

With that resolve, Ellie went into the house to enjoy the evening with her family. It was only as she was alone in her room later that her feelings for Reuben came back to haunt her.

She'd have to call Sarah to see when she might be returning. She had to protect her heart. Although it might be too late.

Sunday morning Ellie got up early and went downstairs to help get ready for their company. She wondered if Reuben would come with Ethan. He'd been to church, but he hadn't come visiting on Visiting Day since he'd moved into their church district.

She watched all day for Reuben but he never came. She frowned. Why not? He'd said that he would see her today. Why did he keep himself isolated from the company of friends and neighbors?

Reuben had planned to visit the Stoltzfuses, but Ethan had woken up crying, and it had taken everything in him to soothe his son. His boy had felt warm to the touch, and he'd realized that his son had a fever. Was it because he was cutting teeth? Some didn't believe that teething caused a fever, but he knew better. He remembered when Sarah was a baby and teething. She'd cried and cried, and she'd run a fever. Mam had put her in a cool bath to try to bring it down, but she'd continued to cry as she sat in the cold water. Reuben had felt bad for his baby sister.

Was Ellie upset that he didn't go? He hadn't known what else to do. His son didn't feel well, and his health and happiness had to come first.

Ethan had fallen asleep about an hour ago. His baby cheeks were red from crying, and Reuben's heart broke every time he went in to check on him. He loved his little boy. It had been tough after his wife had died, but he and Ethan were fine. And he was glad to have Ethan in his life. Despite his loss, he had the most precious gift Susanna could ever have given him—their son. It was up to him to make sure Ethan was loved, fed, clothed and well cared for.

His thoughts centered on Ellie, as they had so many times these past couple of weeks. She was good for his son. For him. She'd make a fine wife, but would she accept that he wanted to marry her for Ethan's sake? He couldn't possibly marry for love. He and Ellie were friends. That was a good basis for marriage, wasn't it? But would it be fair to ask her to marry without the prospect of future children?

A lead weight settled in his chest. No, it wouldn't be fair to her at all.

Ellie drove to Reuben's house the next morning. Although it hadn't been discussed, she'd decided that he still needed her to babysit. Yesterday afternoon, she'd approached her father, uncle and cousins about cleaning up Reuben's property. She'd told them she wanted to surprise him, so if any of them were available, would they come and do the work?

To Ellie's discomfort, Jedidiah had stared at her

while she'd explained. And after Daniel, Joseph, her father and her uncle had agreed to come at ten Monday morning, Jedidiah had cornered her alone to talk about her plans.

"Do you think 'tis a *gut* idea to do this, Ellie?"

Ellie had frowned. "Why not?" She drew in a steady breath. "Reuben has too much to do, Jed. If we can do this for him, it will reduce some of the stress in his life."

Jed had eyed her thoughtfully. "You like him."

"He's my friend."

"Is that all he is?" her cousin had asked softly.

It was all it could ever be. "*Ja*, just friends."

He'd continued to study her a few seconds longer. "*Oll recht.* We'll do what we can to help your…*friend.*"

The sight of Reuben's house brought her back to the present. She drove into his driveway, tied up her horse, then approached the house. Would he tell her why he didn't come over yesterday?

The door opened as she drew closer. "Reuben. You did want me to babysit today, *ja*?"

He nodded. The man appeared exhausted.

"What's wrong?" she asked.

"Ethan's been running a fever. All day yesterday and through the night. I don't know for certain, but I think he may be teething."

Ellie nodded. "*Ja*, teething can be hard on a little one." She studied him thoroughly, then blushed when he held her gaze. "Did you get *any* sleep last night?" Then she felt her face heat even more as she realized how she'd sounded.

"Once he fell asleep."

"Did you give him something to ease his pain?"

"I wasn't sure what to give." He looked regretful, troubled. Helpless.

She smiled. "Don't worry. I'll take care of him for you while you're at work today."

She was happy to see him relax, as if her words had calmed him. "I should go, but…"

"'Tis fine, Reuben. You have work to do. The little man and I will be fine." She walked to the doorway of the great room. "Where is he?"

"Upstairs sleeping. It was a long night."

She handed him a bag. "I fixed you lunch with leftovers from yesterday."

The surprised look on his face warmed her. "*Danki*, Ellie."

"Do you know what time you will be home?"

He stilled. "Do you need to leave at a certain time?"

"*Nay*, I simply wondered, as I thought I'd make a pot roast for supper."

Reuben blinked. "About four or four thirty."

She smiled. "I'll see you then." Ellie watched him through the kitchen window as he climbed into his buggy and left. After he drove away, she went upstairs to check on Ethan.

At nine thirty, two wagons, a buggy and a huge truck drove into the yard. Ellie started. She'd expected everyone at ten. What if Reuben had still been in the area? She stepped outside with Ethan in her arms as Jedidiah climbed down from his wagon.

"You didn't see Reuben, did you?" she asked.

Jed smiled. "I saw him an hour ago but didn't get the chance to speak with him. I stopped by Whittier's Store this morning for some drinks and snacks, and he was there, climbing into the company car that would take him to the job site."

Ellie released a relieved sigh. "What's all this?"

"These are your workers, and this—" he gestured toward the truck "—is a roll-off."

She frowned, then understood as she and Jed watched as the truck released a huge rectangular container near the side of the barn.

"It's for garbage," the young driver said after he'd hopped from his truck to have Jed sign a document attached to a clipboard.

Jed's brothers Daniel and Joseph joined them. Another wagon pulled into the yard that carried her father and Uncle Samuel. To her surprise, her brothers-in-law, Peter, Henry and James, also came to help.

"Danki," she told them.

Her father dismissed her thanks with a wave of his hand. Jedidiah stepped up to be the man in charge. Satisfied that the yard would be cleared before Reuben got home, Ellie headed inside. She had food to prepare— lots of food. Just as she wondered what to make, the side door opened and her cousins' wives, as well as her mother and two of her sisters, entered with a variety of snacks, lunch dishes and desserts.

Ellie beamed at them. They had come because she'd asked. She loved and was grateful for every single one of her family members.

After the work was done, she began to worry about Reuben's reaction when he got home. She tried not to think about how angry he might be once he realized that her family had invaded his kitchen. The room looked wonderful with its new paint and floor. The entire interior was something to be proud of. Reuben had done a great job.

By three thirty everyone had gone, and the roll-away container filled with debris and garbage had been removed. It had been a nice afternoon. Her cousins Daniel and Joseph had finished painting the trim on the front side of the house. Ethan had enjoyed the day, too, she realized. No longer feverish, he had gone willingly to each woman, grinning his baby smile, displaying his two bottom teeth and one up top that recently had broken through. She'd put him down for his nap at one thirty, and despite the commotion out in the yard, he'd fallen asleep immediately.

She heard him in his room now, cooing and making little happy noises. Smiling, Ellie went up to get him. He grinned at her and patted her cheek as she lifted him from his crib. "Did you have a nice nap, *bebe*?" She changed his diaper, then brought him downstairs to help him drink from his cup, then took him outside into the yard to play. She smiled as she kept him company, focusing her attention on him rather than the upcoming confrontation she feared she'd be having with his father. The sun felt warm but the air wasn't humid. She set Ethan on his feet and began to walk him around the yard, held up by her hands.

Reuben was tired. Exhausted, actually. It had been a good workday, but a long one. All he wanted to do was get home, sit down and enjoy a glass of Ellie's iced tea. He'd visit with Ethan, then eat whatever Ellie had left him for supper.

She was an unusual, giving woman. He vaguely wondered what might have happened if he'd courted and married her first. It would have been awkward, he realized, since her older sister Meg had broken off their relationship. But what if he'd never spent time with Meg? What if Ellie had come first? He hadn't realized that Ellie was only a year and a half younger than Meg. He'd thought her much younger.

Would he and Ellie have married? Would Ethan have been Ellie's child? Would they have been happy? Had more children? Because it felt as if Ellie was stronger than Susanna had been at the same age.

Thoughts of his late wife gave him pause. It still hurt to think of her taken from this earth so young...

As he steered his horse home, Reuben looked forward to seeing Ethan and Ellie. It wasn't far to the house. He'd be home by four fifteen.

The first thing he noticed when he pulled into the driveway was Ellie and Ethan seated on a blanket in the yard. Ellie looked breathtaking in pink in the sunlight. Her blond hair looked golden under the summer sun's rays. His son giggled as she tickled him, and her answering laugh was girlish. The sound hit him right in the center of his heart.

And then he saw the yard. He narrowed his gaze. What had happened to all the junk, the garbage, on his property?

Ellie, he thought. Ellie had done this. And after he'd told her he didn't like anyone interfering in his business, in his home. His heart hardened as he headed in her direction. As if sensing him, she glanced over, smiling, until she saw his expression. Her features became shuttered. She lifted Ethan into her arms, propping him on her hip, as she stood. Like she was his mother.

"Elizabeth."

"Reuben," she said. "You're home."

"Obviously."

"And you're mad."

"I'm not happy," he said, his tone even, cold.

"Reuben—"

"You knew how I'd feel about people in my house… *in my yard*." He marveled at the amount of work that had been done in his short absence. *"Helping me."* His gaze wandered to the house. Someone had finished painting the outside window trim. "You're responsible."

He heard her draw a sharp breath. *"Ja."*

Something hurt him inside, cut him deep. "Why?" he snapped.

"Because you have so much to do," she breathed. Her face turned pale. "I wanted to help. My family wanted to help."

"Your family." Surely it had taken more than her father and uncle to accomplish the task.

"My *dat*, *onkel* and cousins," she confessed. She raised her chin in defiance, as if ready to face the brunt of his anger.

The longing he felt for her infuriated him all the more. He had no right to have feelings for her, to notice how pretty she looked or how well she handled his son and had slid easily into his life.

"You should go," he said.

He saw her swallow hard. She nodded. Ellie approached and handed him his son. Then without another word, she walked to her buggy, climbed in and left.

His heart pounded in his chest, making it difficult for him to breathe. She'd meant well, he supposed. She'd known how he felt about accepting help, yet she'd arranged for workers to clear his yard and paint his house.

He grew suddenly anxious as he watched her leave. He called out her name to stop her. Running with Ethan in his arms, he chased after her but she didn't stop. A truck rumbled down the road, drowning out his cries with the loud roar of its engine.

"Ellie!" he cried. He halted, out of breath. She must have heard him, but she'd chosen to ignore him.

Ethan started to cry as if he sensed something was wrong, and Reuben turned his attention to soothing him. "*Ja*, little *soohn*. I know you miss her." *I do, too.*

He had failed too many times in his life. He'd failed and felt helpless when he and Meg had been involved in a buggy accident that had ended up with both of them in the hospital. Ellie's sister had been thrown into the creek. He'd suffered a knot on his head that he later learned was a concussion. He hadn't known how to swim then, and the fact that he hadn't been able to rescue Meg from the water showed him he was a failure.

He'd failed to save his wife, who'd died after giving birth to Ethan. He'd failed to build a new house for him and Ethan. He should be able to handle the renovations to this house and take care of his son, but he'd failed again. He must have, since Ellie had felt the need to step in with her relatives to work on his house and clear his property.

He'd tried. He'd done everything he could to become a better person but his wife had died and his parents had moved away.

It wasn't Ellie's fault that he had trouble accepting help from people. He'd overreacted and hurt Ellie, a woman he cared about, in the process. He'd accepted her help with his son, so what difference did it make if others had come over to assist?

If his life were different, he'd ask Ellie to marry him, but he couldn't. Because of his growing feelings for her. He would always think of Susanna with sadness. She'd had such a short life, and she'd never been able to hold their baby. Yet having Ellie in his life had lessened the loss, had made it bearable. But he wasn't worthy of her.

He should leave Ellie alone. It wasn't fair to her that he couldn't offer her anything but friendship. But yet he couldn't seem to let Ellie go. He would apologize and explain why he felt the way he did.

I can only hope that she understands and forgives me. Because although he didn't deserve her love, he wanted—needed—her friendship.

Chapter Eleven

Ellie went to her room, then placed a call on her cell phone to Sarah. She had to know when the girl was coming back. As much as she cared for Reuben, she had a hard time handling his changing moods. They had been getting along well…until the moment he'd realized what she'd done. She'd known she'd be risking his anger when she arranged to have the work done without his consent. But she'd hoped that afterward, he'd realize a lessening of his burden. She'd only wanted to make his life easier. *Wrong move.*

Someone picked up the phone in the store where Sarah used the phone.

"Hallo?" She gave her name and asked the person to have Sarah call her. The man at the other end of the line agreed to give Sarah the message.

Ellie rattled off her cell number, then hung up. She sat on her bed, feeling hurt and lost. She would no longer be caring for Ethan. *And his father.*

She lay back and closed her eyes. The image of Reuben's livid expression made her gasp and roll over to bury her face into her quilted bed covering. *What have I done?*

Her cell phone rang, startling her. She sat up and answered.

"Ellie!" It was Sarah. Ellie felt relief at hearing from her friend. "How are you? How are Reuben and Ethan? Is everything *oll recht*?"

"*Ja*, Sarah, everything is fine. And your *bruder* and nephew are well. How are you? How is your *mudder*?"

"I'm well, Ellie. Mam is doing better, but she still needs my help with cleaning and with my *grosseldre*." She paused. "I'm sorry, but I can't come back yet."

"That's fine, Sarah. You stay and be there for your *mam* and your grandparents." She knew what it was like to worry about a parent. She worried for hers, wanted to be there for both parents after Charlie married Nate.

"Tell me more about Reuben and Ethan."

"They are both well. Ethan got a new tooth! That makes three, and there's another trying to break through. The house is coming along. Reuben painted the walls and installed new flooring in the kitchen and the gathering room."

Sarah made a sound of pleasure. "I bet everything looks nice."

Ellie couldn't help but smile. "It does."

"Give them my love? I just stopped in for a few things for supper and discovered you'd called. I need to get back to the *haus*."

"I hope your *mudder* feels much better soon, Sarah. Take care."

"I will, Ellie, and *danki*. I feel better knowing that you are there for Ethan and my *bruder*."

Ellie hung up the phone, her thoughts in turmoil. She

had promised to take care of Ethan and to help Reuben, but the man was angry and no longer wanted her help. What was she going to do? She'd have to arrange for someone to care for Ethan. It would be difficult knowing that some other woman would be caring for Reuben's son, making the man his dinner.

She fought the urge to cry. It was her own fault. She lay back on her bed and stared at the ceiling until her eyes blurred with tears.

Reuben was nervous as he raised a hand to knock on the door to the Arlin Stoltzfus residence. Would Ellie agree to see him? Or would she turn him away? Would her parents glare at him with irritation or worse for hurting their daughter? He rapped hard twice.

The door opened, and to his amazement, Missy Stoltzfus's eyes lit up at the sight of him. "Reuben!" she cried. "And Ethan. Come in. Come in! You must be here to see Ellie."

He nodded. "*Ja*, I'd like to speak with her if I may."

"Of course." She gazed at him and Ethan with warmth. "Ellie is in the barn. May I watch Ethan for you while you visit?"

His eyes widened. "You don't mind?"

Ellie's mother held out her arms. "Why would I mind taking care of this precious boy?"

Reuben handed her his son. "*Danki.* I won't be long."

Missy smiled. "Take your time. Ethan and I will get reacquainted."

He headed out to the barn. Inside the light was dim, but he knew exactly where she was. He could detect her sweet scent, felt her presence as his breathing spiked.

Would she see him, then send him away? Or would she listen to his apology and forgive him?

Reuben approached without her notice, watching as she lovingly groomed a horse. She looked pensive, wistful. And sad. Because of him? She was beautiful. He loved everything about her. He stiffened with the realization, briefly closed his eyes, then moved to the door of the stall.

"Ellie."

She gasped as if she'd recognized his voice but didn't immediately turn around. "Why are you here, Reuben?"

"I need to talk with you."

She spun, speared him with a hostile glance. He drew a sharp breath as he felt the sting of her anger. "Where's Ethan?"

"With your *mudder*." He saw her mouth gape open in shock. "Ellie, I've come to apologize. To explain." He heard her draw a calming breath.

"Explain what?"

"Why I have trouble accepting help from others." He didn't like admitting his failures, but he would because Ellie meant something to him. It scared him, these sharp, painful feelings he had for her. He gazed at her with longing. She had turned back to grooming her horse. "I've felt like a failure for a long time," he began.

Her hand holding the brush stilled. She faced him and regarded him with a soft expression. "Why, Reuben?" she asked quietly.

"You know that Meg and I were in a buggy accident. I didn't save her. I couldn't have saved her. I didn't know how to swim." He looked away, unwilling to see her censure, but she had to know the truth. That her sister would have died if Peter hadn't arrived and rescued her.

"You didn't cause the accident," she murmured.

He shot her a glance. To his amazement, she didn't appear to be upset by his admission. "And my wife... she died, Ellie, because I wanted a family. There was nothing I could do for her. Nothing."

"You felt helpless." She gazed at him with blue eyes filled with emotion.

Pity? He didn't want her pity. But he realized that she didn't pity him. It was compassion he recognized in her gaze.

"*Ja*, I felt helpless." He paused. "I wasn't a *gut* father to Ethan after Susanna died. I was wrapped up with anger and feeling sorry for myself so I let my mother and sister care for him."

He saw something shift across her expression. A look of sadness? Disappointment? She couldn't be any more disappointed in him than he was in himself. *I'm not* gut *enough for her.*

"Grief, Reuben. You were grieving." Her study of him made him glance away. He needed to go on and couldn't bear to see her face change.

"I've watched you with Ethan," she continued. "You're a *gut* and loving *vadder*."

"I wasn't."

"But you are now," she replied, once again surprising him. She gazed at him thoughtfully. "You need to get past the determination that you have to do everything yourself. You belong to a community. We help each other. There is no shame in asking for or accepting help. If you don't accept help from your fellow church members, how can we ask for yours?"

Reuben was startled. "You think someone would want my help?"

She frowned. "Didn't members of your former church community help each other?"

He'd been so wrapped up in the things that had happened to him in the last few years, he had forgotten, but he must have. "I'm not a *gut* man."

"Reuben Miller, you don't get to judge you. Only the Lord can judge, and I believe He loves you and looks upon you kindly. I believe you are a *gut* man." She stepped closer. Terrified by his feelings, he instinctively backed away. She didn't follow. The hurt look on her face twisted something painfully inside him.

"You have friends who want to help you," Ellie said huskily. "Learn to use your friends. They won't mind. I can promise you."

"*Ja.* I've been worried for so long that I haven't been able to see past the work and my need to be self-reliant. I've pushed everyone away." He hesitated. "Except you." He flashed her a twisted smile. "Actually, I have pushed you away a bit," he admitted, "which is why I'm here. To change that."

"You're willing to accept my help," she murmured, her tone off, as she spun back to grooming the horse, slow even strokes of the brush against the animal's chestnut coat.

"Ellie," he said, "I know that I have much to be thankful for. My son. A place to live—although it still needs work. But not as much anymore thanks to you." His voice trailed off and he felt something close to... despair. She didn't turn, wouldn't meet his gaze. Had she given up on him? Had she decided that she'd had enough and washed her hands of him? He couldn't go until he made her understand. "I overreacted," he whispered. "I'm sorry."

Her hand stopped mid brush stroke. She faced him. "I understand that things have been hard for you, Reuben, but we—my family and I—weren't trying to undermine you. We just wanted to help. You shouldn't have to do everything on your own."

His chest tightened as he held her gaze. If only things were different…if he'd married her first, there wouldn't have been a problem, he thought again. Unless she'd died the way that Susanna had after giving birth to his child. The thought made him shudder and sent a shaft of pain into his chest and his heart. "I know."

"Do you?"

He inclined his head. "I do." He debated whether to tell her more and decided that he owed it to her. "I once told you that when I marry again, it will be so that Ethan can have a mother." He paused. "I still want that."

She blinked without saying a word.

He was silent for several seconds as he continued to stare at her. "What I never admitted to you was that I noticed you first. Before I became involved with Meg." He hesitated before continuing. "I avoided you because I felt you were too young for marriage. You had years to enjoy before becoming a wife and a mother. Meg's attention was flattering at a time I wanted to wed." He saw disbelief then pain in her eyes before she shut down her expression. "I liked Meg, and I was hurt when she broke things off to be with Peter."

"I don't want to hear—"

"Ellie, please," he pleaded. "Let me finish."

Closing her eyes, she gave a nod. She obviously didn't want to hear about his feelings for her sister. Which lifted his spirits. And gave him hope.

"Susanna and I met not long after your sister and I

parted ways. We liked each other immediately. We became friends." He watched Ellie carefully to gauge her reaction. "We wanted the same thing—to get married and have a family and a home..."

"Why are you telling me this?" she asked sharply.

"I need you to understand why I've been determined to do things on my own."

"Reuben—"

He gave her a tentative smile. "Ellie."

"Why do I need to know?"

"So that you'll know the truth...and maybe forgive me?"

Ellie didn't want to hear about the other women who had been in Reuben's life. She already understood why he had difficulty accepting help, but she meant it when she told him he needed to get over it.

He'd noticed her before Meg? *Unlikely.* Or could it be true? Why was he telling her this? Wrapped up in her thoughts and the pain of his rejection, she felt her mind drift and she withdrew from him as she tried to protect herself.

"Ellie?"

She met his gaze. "You want me to continue to watch Ethan," she said crisply. He would allow her to watch his son, cook his meals and clean his house. *Like a stand-in wife.* She'd be useful until he found a woman he decided to marry, then she'd be on her own.

He blinked as if stunned by her tone. *"Ja."*

"I'll come back to watch your son, but under my terms."

Looking wary, Reuben tilted his blond head as he studied her. "What terms?"

"If I want to bring Ethan here to the house, I should be allowed to take him."

He nodded in agreement, and a little smile tilted up the corners of his mouth.

Ellie narrowed her gaze. "If I want my cousins to help with your house, then you need to be amicable." His brow furrowed. She could tell he didn't like that.

"Fine," he said reluctantly, quietly. But she knew he felt uneasy with the idea.

"Gut." Her head ached, and Ellie lifted a hand to rub one temple. "Why tell me about Meg and Susanna? So I'll feel bad enough to return?"

"Nay. I just wanted you to understand..." He shifted and looked away.

She tried to gauge his thoughts. "Reuben?"

"I care about you, Ellie."

She jerked. "As friends," she murmured. "I know."

He nodded. "I wish it could be more."

So did she. Ellie had had enough of this conversation. It hurt when he confirmed he was unwilling to pursue a relationship with her. *I'm gut enough to be his friend but nothing more.* She swallowed against a suddenly tight throat and changed the subject. "I spoke with Sarah today. Your *mudder* still needs her help for a few more weeks." She watched him closely. "Did you talk with her?"

Was that why he'd wanted to apologize? So that she would help him until Sarah returned? Her lips twisted. She'd been pushing him to accept help, and now that he was willing, she wanted more from him.

"Nay, we haven't spoken," he replied quietly. He gazed at her with an odd look in his beautiful blue eyes that made her heart race. "Ellie, it doesn't mat-

ter if my sister is coming back or not. This isn't about Ethan or Sarah."

"Then what is it about, Reuben?"

He looked suddenly uncomfortable. "I was wondering if…"

"I told you I'll take care of Ethan. Isn't that what you want?"

Reuben's face turned red. She frowned. She'd never seen him embarrassed before, but now she knew she was right in believing that he'd come to make sure he had a babysitter for his son. "Ellie—"

"I'll see you tomorrow, Reuben." She turned her back on him to finish grooming the mare.

"Ellie, you were too young years ago," he whispered, "but you're not now."

She froze but didn't face him.

"I've thought about asking you to marry me—not for Ethan but for me."

She couldn't help turning then. His expression was anguished. She had the strongest urge to take him into her arms and hold him tightly. Reassure him that they would be wonderful together. But, of course, she didn't. "Reuben—"

"I can't, though. Don't you see?" He ran his hand raggedly through his blond hair. "I care too much for you. If we wed, I'll lose you, too."

"Reuben—"

"*Nay*, Ellie," he breathed. He touched her arm, and she felt the warmth of him beneath the fabric. "I wish…"

"What do you wish?" she breathed huskily.

"*Nay!*" he gasped. Then he turned and hurriedly left, as if he couldn't bear to stay.

Ellie watched him, her heart racing wildly. Everything in her longed to run after him. But she didn't. Because she knew that he meant it. He would never marry her because he wouldn't marry for love.

She frowned. He'd never actually admitted loving her. If he had, she would have chased him until he gave in to his feelings. But he didn't love her. Ellie closed her eyes and released a shuddering breath. She had fallen in love with him. With him and his son. And except for a temporary babysitter for Ethan, she would never be anything more than a fellow church member. She didn't think they'd remain friends after Sarah's return when he no longer needed her. And that hurt and felt wrong.

She stood for a moment, her heart aching. She was empty inside, and the void hurt. She would be his friend, watch his son and find someone to take her place as the boy's caretaker before her heart broke beyond repair.

Again, the sudden urge to run after him overtook her. Ellie put away the brush and raced toward the house, but Reuben had gone. He must have rushed in to grab his son and escaped.

She would see him tomorrow. She'd promised that she'd be there for Ethan. Ellie would take her cue from Reuben then. If he acted like they'd never had this conversation, then she would pretend that she hadn't been affected by it. She blinked back tears, then entered the house.

"Ellie," her mother said warmly. "Ethan is such a sweet boy. No wonder you enjoy taking care of him."

Ellie nodded. "He is. Did you see his newest tooth?"

"I did." She frowned. "I'm sorry Reuben had to leave so quickly. He said he had things to do, but he thanked me for watching the boy while you talked." Mam narrowed her gaze as she studied Ellie. "What did you talk about?"

"About Ethan. He wanted to make sure I'll be there tomorrow," she said truthfully. There was no reason for her mother to know everything they'd discussed. "Do you need me to do anything for you tomorrow before I go? I know you wanted to can tomatoes."

"Meg and Leah will be here. There is nothing to stop you from helping Reuben."

"Meg's home." Ellie managed a smile. "I hadn't realized she and Peter had returned from New Wilmington."

"They'll be staying for supper, so you'll get a chance to visit with them then."

"If you change your mind and need help tomorrow, let me know. I can always bring Ethan home with me."

"As much as I enjoy seeing him, Meg will have her little one, and I'll want to focus on having time with him." She grinned. "But if you decide you want to come home tomorrow, please do. But not to work. We'll be done by then."

"Ethan usually naps in the afternoon, but maybe I'll bring him another morning." *If I'll still be watching him then.* "May I help with supper?" She managed to distract her mother away from talking about Reuben or Ethan any further.

Her conversation with Reuben had left Ellie aching and confused. And longing for something that would never be.

Chapter Twelve

The next morning Ellie filled her buggy's backseat with food supplies. As she started to climb into the vehicle, she heard the sound of wheels on the dirt drive to their farmhouse. She recognized the pony cart's driver immediately.

"Ellie."

"Rebecca!"

Rebecca Troyer, the young Amish woman who'd been handling her clients for over a week, approached with a look of regret that gave Ellie a bad feeling.

"I'm sorry for the early morning visit, but I had to tell you I can no longer work at your clients' homes for you. I've been feeling overwhelmed."

Ellie nodded. "I appreciate all you've done. Can you handle today's?"

"There are none today. The Broderick woman canceled, and the Smiths didn't like the way I cleaned for them last week, although I spent extra time at their house and I never charged them for it."

The Smiths had been difficult on occasion, and Ellie thought she'd cut them loose, but they must have gotten Rebecca's number. "The Smiths are no longer my clients."

Rebecca frowned. "I didn't realize. When the woman called, I thought she was one of yours."

"Used to be, but to say the family is difficult is an understatement." The only client she was worried about was Olivia Broderick, the woman fighting cancer. "*Danki* for what all you've done."

The young Amish woman smiled. "The extra money was appreciated. I wish I could still help. It's been tough meshing the schedules since some of yours wanted me to come when I already had others scheduled that day."

"I understand," Ellie said. "I'll make other arrangements. Nothing to worry about."

Her friend looked relieved. "Enjoy your day, Ellie."

"The same to you, Rebecca." Ellie watched her leave before she left for Reuben's. She had to decide what do. Did she find someone else to clean for her or find another caretaker for Ethan? Would Reuben be relieved if she found another caretaker for his son?

She thought of their conversation in the barn. He had confessed that he was drawn to her, but she didn't believe he felt anything but gratitude toward her.

She had liked her housecleaning business, but she hadn't missed it recently. Sarah wouldn't return for a long while yet. *Do I want someone else to take care of Ethan?* She inhaled sharply. *Nay, I don't.* But if she gave up her business, then what happened when she was no longer needed by Reuben?

She frowned. It wasn't as if she needed the money. She'd been saving for years now. She had a nice nest egg in the bank. And Charlie was getting married in November. She wouldn't be housecleaning outside her parents' house then. Did it matter if she gave it up now rather than later? A little boy needed her. She wanted to be there for him. And for Reuben. She'd always known that it was a temporary arrangement. He wouldn't need her once his sister returned.

Ellie sighed. She had the distinct feeling that after their conversation last night, Reuben would look harder for a wife. Someone safe, who didn't mind a marriage of convenience.

She shuddered out a breath. "If he falls in love with the woman he marries, I'll have to watch." *Broken-hearted.*

Ellie had made up her mind. She would shut down her business. She'd ask Rebecca if she wanted her clients permanently. The woman could change the schedule any way she wanted to make it work out for her.

Ellie realized that she felt slightly afraid of her decision, but she wouldn't change her mind. There was much to do at home, and if she was to be there for her parents after Charlie married, she would be ready.

She caught sight of Reuben waiting at the side door for her when she arrived. Her heart began to thump hard. Would she ever get over this heightened sensation of expectancy whenever he was near?

She took care of her buggy and grabbed her things from the back, then headed toward the house. Ellie felt like a bundle of nerves by the time she reached the house. When her gaze locked with Reuben's, she offered a tentative smile. He grinned as if happy to see her, and she relaxed and returned his grin.

"Ellie," he murmured as he opened the door for her and stepped aside for her to enter. Reuben looked wonderful in a blue short-sleeved shirt, black suspenders and black tri-blend pants. As she entered, she noticed his bare feet, and something inside her shifted.

Ethan was in his high chair and she immediately went to him. "*Hallo*, little one."

The little boy looked up and his small mouth split in a drooling smile. He made a gurgling sound of delight. Ellie unstrapped him from his chair and tugged him into her arms. She hugged him and nuzzled her nose into his neck. Ethan giggled and she nuzzled again. Each time she did it, the child laughed, clearly delighted with her attention.

She felt Reuben's presence behind her. She faced him and was stunned to see warmth and caring in his beautiful blue eyes.

"You're great with him, Ellie," he said softly as he sat in a kitchen chair to put on his socks and shoes.

"He's an easy child."

"*Nay*, I think 'tis you." The affection in his gaze changed the color of his eyes to deep blue.

"Reuben—"

"*Danki*, Ellie," he breathed.

"There's no need—"

"I've been thinking all night," he admitted. He stood and closed the gap between them. His physical nearness caused a tiny fluttering in her belly. "I've been thinking about you…and me. And there is something I'd like to ask you." He hesitated. "Ellie Stoltzfus, will you marry me?"

She started. *"What?"*

"I would like you to be my wife," he said softly. "You'll make Ethan a wonderful *mudder* and me…"

Mother. Every other word he'd said after that one was lost. Because she could focus on only one thing.

Reuben needed a mother for his son, and he'd decided that it should be her. Because she was good with Ethan. She felt the blood drain from her face. He wouldn't have asked her if he loved her. Which meant he didn't.

Ellie swallowed hard. She loved him. If he'd loved her even just a little, she would have happily married him. But she wouldn't—couldn't—be a mother and not a real wife.

"That's…unexpected." Ellie put distance between them. She drew in a sharp breath, then released it. "*Nay*, I'm sorry but I can't marry you."

He blinked. *"Nay?"* He appeared stunned. "You don't want to be my wife?" He looked upset. Defeated. As if her refusal had shaken him. Roughly.

She opened her mouth to tell him she loved him but then closed it. He was grateful for her help. His proposal had been impulsive, she realized, sprung from his gratitude.

He looked stunned. Then, as if coming to his senses, he wiped his face of all expression.

"Do you want to know why I can't marry you, Reuben?" she asked, watching him closely. When he nodded, she said, "I want a family with someone who loves me."

Reuben paled.

She nodded. "Just as I thought. I'm sorry but I won't marry you. The man I marry will love me and want to have children with me."

Darkness descended on his features as he took a step closer. "Ellie… I can't."

Ellie smiled weakly. "I know. Let's keep things how they've been. Leave our arrangement as it stands until Sarah gets back." She felt her words like knife stabs into her heart. She wouldn't accept anything less than what her sisters had with their husbands—men who loved and wanted babies with their wives.

He gave a sharp nod. As he turned away, he ran a hand through his blond hair, mussing it into gorgeous disarray. Her heart hurt as she watched him. She wanted a life with him, but she wouldn't accept anything less than a life with love and a passel of children.

He grabbed a paper bag off the countertop. His lunch, she realized, that he must have made himself. He wouldn't need her for much longer. In a few weeks, his sister would return and she'd be back at home with her parents.

She stood in the doorway with Ethan on her hip, watching Reuben as he left for work. He headed toward his buggy, then paused midstride to glance back at her. There was nothing in his expression to give away his thoughts. "Not to worry, Reuben Miller," she said with what she hoped was a smile, "Ethan's safe with me."

He gave her a nod. Minutes later, he met her gaze and waved briefly as he steered his buggy off the property. Ellie felt her composure slip as she fought back tears.

Yet she managed a smile for Ethan. "'Tis just you and me, little man," she murmured as she opened the door and slipped inside. It was only after she put Ethan down for his nap that she allowed herself to cry. After a few minutes, her tears drying on her cheeks, she cleaned Reuben's house while his son slept.

He couldn't do it, Reuben thought as he drove to work. He couldn't marry and get her with child. There were ways to prevent children, weren't there? He cared for Ellie more than he'd cared for anyone in a long while. But to wed, then get her with child? *Nay*. How could he?

Did he want to marry Ellie? *Ja*. Because he wanted a mother for his son? Yes, she was wonderful with him. But that wasn't the only reason. He loved her. He thought about her all night long and knew he was hopelessly in love with Ellie Stoltzfus.

He knew now he couldn't have her. She wanted children. She loved Ethan. It was easy to see how much in her blue gaze. But she wanted more. And he couldn't give them to her. Because if he did, then something might happen to her. And he couldn't risk it. He wouldn't survive if anything bad happened to Ellie. He'd have to look for a woman who didn't want children, who'd be content with Ethan. Someone older who couldn't have children, perhaps.

Even if it wasn't Ellie.

He inhaled sharply as he was hit by a fresh wave of pain.

Ellie was a good friend. He had to be satisfied with her friendship.

Reuben arrived at Yoder's Craft Shop and General Store, where he'd be meeting his crew. They would be driven via car by their English crew member. As he went around the back of the store to where Henry and Leah Yoder allowed them to park their buggies, he saw that Rob Brandon was already there, waiting with the Suburban the construction company provided for their transportation. The three other Amish workers were there, getting their tools out of their buggies. Reuben pulled in his wagon, then got up, secured his horse and reached in for his tool belt. He addressed Rob. "Everyone here?"

The twenty-year-old driver nodded. "All here and accounted for, boss man."

Reuben sighed at the young man's irreverence. Rob was a careful driver and a hard worker. He didn't have any real problems with him. "Let's move."

While everyone got into the car with their tools, he couldn't keep his thoughts from Ellie. A band of pain tightened around his chest. He breathed through it, and the constriction faded.

The job was a new one. They would be building a house for a client of the company, starting from the bottom up. Last week, the basement was dug and footers poured. Today Reuben would be overseeing the masonry work. The property was large, and Reuben told the driver to park away from the building area. He climbed out with his crew, grabbed his tools and went to work.

The end of the workday came faster than he thought it would. He stood for a few moments, talking with the crew, deciding what they wanted to accomplish the next day. Afterward, as he climbed into the vehicle, he was left alone with his thoughts of Ellie. He'd tried fighting them all day, but her image—and her rejection— wouldn't let go of him.

While Ethan slept, the day dragged on. Everywhere Ellie looked in the house, she saw Reuben. Reuben eating at the kitchen table. Reuben in the great room holding his son. The images, the memories, were painful. She decided that she'd take Ethan to see her parents. She'd hoped that her mother and sisters would have finished canning by the time they arrived. She had to get away from the Reuben Miller home. The morning had started well, but then after the man's marriage proposal, things had ended badly.

She loved Reuben, she did, but she would not marry him with the knowledge that he'd never love her in the same way. It was good that she'd said no. It was the only thing she could do under the circumstances, but it devastated her.

By the time she arrived home, her sisters had left and her mother was enjoying a cup of tea alone at the kitchen table. "Mam," she greeted.

Her mother smiled. "Ellie! And little Ethan."

"I'd hoped that I wouldn't be interrupting."

"As you can see, you're not." Mam gestured toward a chair at the kitchen table. "Sit. Tea?"

Ellie nodded. "*Ja*, please." She pulled a high chair from the corner of the kitchen to the table and strapped Ethan in. She sprinkled the tray with cereal.

Without asking, her mother filled a child's sippy cup with apple juice, which she silently put on the table. Ellie smiled, then gave it to Ethan. She grinned as the boy put the cup to his lips and drank. He gave her a sloppy smile as he set it down, then grabbed a handful of cereal.

After enjoying tea, then lunch with her mother a little while later, she headed back. Reuben and his marriage proposal had been on her mind all day. She was nervous about facing him. The last thing she wanted was for him to realize that she had deep feelings for him.

Ellie glanced at her watch. She'd get home before Reuben's return.

As much as she loved the little boy in the seat beside her, she wanted children of her own. *At least three more.* She thought of the women within the community.

Any number of them could marry Reuben, especially the older spinsters. Drawing a painful breath, Ellie realized she hated the thought of him with anyone but her. But how could she complain if he chose another when she'd said no? Which gave her something to think about, something bound to keep her up in the nights ahead.

When they arrived, Ellie was surprised to see Reuben's buggy in the yard. Her heart raced and she felt sick to her stomach. Heat filled her cheeks, and she had the strongest urge to flee. But then Ethan made a sound, and she realized that she couldn't escape, not with the man's son.

There was no sign of Reuben in the yard or inside near the window as they approached the house. Forcing herself to relax, Ellie turned the doorknob, only to have the door pulled from her hand. Reuben stood on the threshold, looking tired and disheveled. She fought the strongest urge to hug him.

"Reuben," she greeted. "We went on a little trip to see my *eldre*."

"Did you have a nice visit?"

"We did," she said as she smiled at the child in her arms. "Didn't we, little man?" When she turned back to Reuben, a strange look passed across his face. "Are you hungry? I thought you'd be home later or we would have come back sooner."

"'Tis fine, Ellie." He stepped back and she lowered Ethan to the new kitchen floor to play.

"I made chicken potpie earlier, enough for you to have dinner for two days. And there is a cherry pie in the pantry. I remember Sarah said that you liked it. If not, there are cookies in a tin beside the pie." Ellie knew that she was babbling but was unable to stop herself.

Her love for him made her nervous. "I can make you something else if you'd like."

"Ellie."

"There is plenty of meat in the freezer, and I took out ground beef earlier to make you something different for dinner tomorrow."

"Ellie." His quiet voice drew her up.

"Ja?"

"'Tis all fine. I appreciate all that you do for me." He smiled. *"Relax and breathe."* He looked amused, which only added to his good looks and angered her that she felt embarrassed.

"I should go." She bent down and placed a gentle kiss on little Ethan's head. When she rose, she found Reuben watching her with strong emotion in his eyes. She glanced away, because she had to be reading him wrong. It looked as if he didn't want to lose her. But she knew that couldn't be true—he only wanted to marry so that Ethan could have a mother. Any woman who was good with children would do. "I'll see you tomorrow, Reuben—" She stopped. "Unless you arranged to have someone else come in my place?"

He shook his blond head, his blue gaze continuing his perusal of her. The feelings churning inside fueled her need to escape. After a smile for the child on the floor, Ellie opened the door and stepped outside. She made it to her buggy before she glanced back toward the house. Reuben was there. "Ellie!" he cried.

She froze.

"Please think about it. Marrying me. *Please* reconsider and think about it."

Ellie nodded, for what else could she do? She felt a

pang in her heart as he held her gaze. Her thoughts were filled with his marriage proposal as she headed home.

That night while lying in bed, Ellie stared at the ceiling. She loved Reuben. Should she have agreed to marry him? Wasn't it better to marry someone you loved than not marry at all? Would she ever find love with another? Or was Reuben *it* for her? She covered her eyes with an arm. What was she going to do? She loved Ethan, but to be a wife and mother without love? The thought was too painful, and she tried to push it away.

Chapter Thirteen

Ellie received a call from Olivia Broderick the next morning. The woman's plea for her to clean her house this morning aroused her sympathy for the ill woman, and she agreed. After she hung up the phone, she went in search of her sister and asked Charlie if she could watch Ethan.

"*Ja*, I can babysit for him this morning," Charlie said, her expression soft after hearing about the woman's situation.

"*Danki*," Ellie murmured. "I'll relieve you as soon as I'm done."

Ellie headed to the Broderick house, aware that she'd miss seeing Reuben before he left for work. What would he think when Charlie showed up in her place? That she was purposely ignoring him?

Ellie had to hide her shock when Olivia Broderick opened the door. The poor woman looked awful, with sunken cheeks and deep, dark circles around her eyes. She had lost a lot of weight, judging by how thin and bony she appeared.

"Mrs. Broderick," she greeted softly. The woman

stepped back and Ellie entered with her cleaning supplies. "You're not feeling well."

Olivia shook her head. "The chemo treatments have been hard, but I'm hanging in there." She tried to smile. "Thank you for coming on such short notice." She frowned. "I didn't know this Rebecca who called to schedule."

"She's a friend who does a good job. You can trust her with your house."

"You want to get out of the business," the woman said astutely.

Ellie inclined her head. "My sister's getting married soon, and I want to be available for my parents."

"Are they ill?"

"No, but they're getting older, and they can't do as much as they used to. I'll be the only one home to help." Ellie hesitated. "And I've been helping a friend with a child. The friend works and I babysit."

Olivia seemed to understand. "I'm sorry if I pulled you away. I trust you. I can't keep up with the house at all anymore. I need someone to clean frequently."

"I think you should give Rebecca a try, but I'm here now, and I'll come back next week until you are satisfied with my replacement."

"You'll call Rebecca for me? Ask her to stop in to talk with me?"

"I'll be happy to." Ellie paused. "Perhaps we'll clean together next week and you'll see what I mean."

Four hours later, Ellie finished the Broderick residence and left to relieve Charlie. She'd done more work than usual, with Olivia unable to do the simplest household tasks.

She arrived two hours before Reuben was due home.

Charlie grinned as Ethan leaned out of her arms and reached for Ellie. "He loves that you're here. I think he's becoming attached to you."

Ellie frowned. "That might not be *gut* for him."

"Why not?"

"Sarah will be back soon, and I won't be coming anymore."

"You could stop by to clean for them," Charlie said.

She shook her head. "I think not."

"Why not?"

"It just wouldn't be wise," Ellie insisted.

Charlie fixed her with a look, but dropped the topic of conversation. She gave Ellie an overview of her time with Ethan.

"Was Reuben upset that I hadn't come?"

Her sister shrugged. "I think he was surprised to see me, but he seemed *oll recht* after I told him you had to work this morning."

Ethan patted her cheek, and Ellie grinned at him. "Did he nap?" she asked her sister.

"*Ja.* Had a nice one this morning. He just woke up from a shorter one this afternoon." Charlie reached out to caress the little boy's cheek. "I think he wants a snack. He didn't eat much for lunch."

"I'll make him one." She smiled her thanks. "I appreciate your help."

"I didn't mind. Nate is shopping for building supplies out of town this morning. I'll head over to the *haus* to see if he's back."

"I'll see you at home later," Ellie said.

Charlie assured her that she would, then she left. With Ethan firmly on her left hip, she went to the pantry. Ethan seemed to have grown a great deal in the last two weeks. His second upper tooth had broken through, leaving him with four teeth total. It was time to introduce him to new foods. She eyed the pantry shelves as she debated what to give him.

The sound of the side entrance door drew her from the food closet. To her shock, Reuben was home early. He stopped and stared when he realized that she and not Charlie was holding his son. "Ellie."

"*Hallo*, Reuben. I didn't expect you home for a while yet."

"I didn't expect to see you today." An odd, undecipherable look flickered across his expression. "Charlie said you had to work."

Ellie nodded. Was he upset with her decision to take the job? She debated whether to explain, but when his lips firmed, she decided not to bother. She had the right to choose what she wanted to do for the day. It wasn't as if she'd left him without a babysitter. She'd arranged for Charlie to take her place.

She sniffed and turned away. "I was going to get Ethan a snack," she said stiffly. "Do you want anything?"

Reuben didn't answer. He stared at her as she strapped Ethan into his chair. When she met his gaze, she shifted uncomfortably under his steady regard.

"I'll get Ethan a snack, then I'll leave you two alone."

He seemed to come out of a trance. He reached out to snag her gently by the arm. "Don't leave yet. I'm sorry if I seemed rude. 'Tis been a rough day..."

She felt herself soften. "Why don't you sit and I'll get you a tall glass of iced tea and a piece of cake?"

The man smiled. "That would be nice. *Danki*." Ellie

tilted her head as she looked from the boy to his father. "Keep him company?"

He nodded. As she poured him some iced tea, she heard Reuben chatting with his son, telling him about his day.

Ellie felt his eyes on her, assessing, before she entered the walk-in pantry. She grabbed an unopened bag of cereal and returned to father and son.

Reuben was silent as she opened the bag and spread a handful of puffed rice on his son's tray. Ethan picked up a piece of cereal, put it in his mouth and chewed happily.

She cut Reuben a piece of cake. "Will you be fine on your own? If so, I'll leave—"

"Please don't go." He caught her arm again, and she froze as the warmth of his touch radiated along her skin.

"Reuben."

"Spend some time with me, Ellie. *Please*." His eyes begged. "You said yourself that you didn't expect me home. Please stay and keep me company."

Gazing at him, she debated. She wanted to stay with a strength of will that shocked her, but she was afraid. She'd already fallen for this man. To spend more time with him could ultimately wound her deeply in the end.

Her will overcame her protective sense. "I can stay a little while," she murmured. The relief on his features was startling. "Are you hungry?"

He shook his head. *"Nay."* He watched her as she put away the cake. "Would you go on a picnic with me and Ethan?"

"Reuben—"

"Please."

She couldn't resist him. It was already too late. Her heart was involved and would suffer later. Until then, she'd enjoy every second with her two favorite men outside of family. "I don't think we have picnic food in the refrigerator."

"You'll come? Stay for supper?" He looked hopeful, like a little boy.

Ellie smiled. "I'll come, but—"

"I'll go to the store. What would you like? Fried chicken? Potato salad?"

She laughed. "Get whatever you'd like. There's nothing I won't eat."

Reuben rose with a pleased look. "I'll be right back."

"I thought you said you weren't hungry."

"I suddenly got my appetite back!" He opened the door to leave.

"Reuben!" she called. He shot her a look as if he expected her to change her mind, and he anticipated disappointment. "You didn't eat your cake. I brought it this afternoon. If you're okay with the chocolate cake, we'll have it for dessert."

He grinned. "I love chocolate cake," he said.

Then he left, and Ellie found herself grinning, surprised with how eager he seemed to be about spending time with her.

Reuben was excited as he drove his horse and buggy to Whittier's Store. Ellie had agreed to go on a picnic with him! He'd never before felt this wild expectancy. He shouldn't have asked her to marry him the way he had. He wanted her for his wife and Ethan's mother. He should have courted her before asking. He knew the problem of children still hung between them, but they'd figure it out.

The memory of the first time he'd seen Ellie came

to mind. She was sweet and young, with a pretty face and lovely blue eyes. She'd worn a pale blue dress that heightened her coloring. He'd fought his attraction to her because he'd thought her too young. Her older sister Meg was warm, open and dark-haired. The complete opposite of Ellie in looks but not in temperament. Meg's interest had buoyed his spirits and bolstered his self-esteem at a time when he'd needed it. Until the accident and Peter Zook.

He sighed as he pulled into the store parking lot. Things happened for a reason. Reuben prayed daily for strength and guidance. He believed that he and Ellie were meant to be together, that their relationship was blessed by God.

He bought fried chicken that looked crispy and smelled delicious, a quart of potato salad—Amish style—some broccoli salad, a half-dozen freshly baked rolls and a six-pack of root beer. He hoped she liked root beer. If not, they'd bring iced tea. He paid for the items and headed for home, eager and excited.

Worry set in as he drove closer to the house. He'd have to be careful; he didn't want to scare her off. He prayed he could convince her that he cared, that his intentions were honorable. He wanted Ellie for himself as much if not more than he wanted her for his son.

It was a perfect evening for a picnic. The temperature was warm. There was a gentle breeze and little humidity. He made Ellie wait inside with Ethan as he chose a spot in the backyard, then spread out a quilt. He retrieved his purchases from his buggy—paper plates and plastic utensils along with a small bouquet of flowers he'd paid for at the last minute. He set out supper and used an old canning jar from the barn for the flowers.

He filled it with water from the outside hand pump in the backyard, then carefully arranged the daisies. He placed her flowers along one edge of the blanket, then headed in to get Ellie and Ethan.

She was seated at the table near Ethan's chair showing him different shapes with her fingers when he walked in. Ethan had no idea what Ellie was doing, but from his giggles, his son clearly loved it. Or he loved her attention.

"Ellie."

She met his gaze with a twinkle of amusement in her pretty blue eyes. "Is supper ready?"

He beamed at her. "*Ja.* Come and see."

She picked up Ethan. As she approached, Reuben held out a hand to her and was surprised when she took it. He led her carefully outside, conscious that he was with his two most precious people.

"Fried chicken, potato and broccoli salad and freshly baked yeast rolls," he announced as they reached the blanket. "But no dessert, for you brought chocolate cake, and I like chocolate cake."

Her smile reached her pretty eyes. "Sounds delicious." Still holding Ethan, her eyes widened as she spotted the flowers. She shot him a surprised look. "Daisies?"

"I thought you would like them." He frowned. "Was I wrong?"

"They're my favorite flower. How did you know?"

He grinned. "I didn't, but you are bright and cheery like a daisy. When I saw them, I immediately thought of you." He heard her sharp intake of breath. She was beautiful, and she'd captured his heart. "Have a seat," he instructed. He reached for Ethan so that she could get comfortable on the quilt, close to the flowers, he noted with delight.

He sat down and set Ethan between them. "I'm glad you stayed," he said huskily.

"Reuben—"

"No pressure, Ellie. I'd simply like to enjoy a meal outside with you."

She was silent a long moment. "Me, too," she whispered so softly he almost didn't hear her. When he realized what she'd said, he felt a rush of warmth and affection. It took all of his control to keep from scooting closer to her. But he stayed where he was. He'd promised he wouldn't pressure her. He'd go slow and take it one step at a time.

They ate companionably, enjoying their meal. Ellie stopped eating frequently to feed Ethan dried cereal and pieces of cut-up peaches that she'd retrieved from the house, along with a baby cookie. She fed him easily, naturally, as if she were his mother. She smiled at his son when she saw that he had peach juice in the corners of his mouth. She picked a napkin and proceeded to wipe his little mouth. Ethan squirmed a bit but allowed her to finish. She rewarded him with a grin and the cookie.

Reuben chatted with her about the weather. Ellie told him about her parents, her sisters and her father's dog. "I never thought I'd see Dat with a dog of his own. After Nell married James and took her dog, my *vadder* seemed lost. He perked up after he decided to get one of his own. It was doing some renovations in a stall for his new dog that helped to bring my sister Leah and her husband Henry together."

"You have four sisters," he said with interest.

She nodded. "We're all close. We enjoy each other's

company. We don't spend as much time together as we used to, but when we do, it's *wunderbor*."

All too soon for Reuben, they had finished their picnic and it was time for Ellie to go home.

"*Danki* for the picnic," Ellie said as she gathered up the remnants of their meal. "And the daisies."

Reuben picked up the empty paper plates and stuffed them inside the paper bag the chicken had come in. "*Danki* for keeping me company…" He wanted to say more but couldn't.

She was quiet. The intensity of her gaze speared through him. "I enjoyed myself." She stood, then reached for Ethan. "I should be able to come tomorrow morning, if you still want me to."

Nodding, he said, "I do." As he followed her toward the house, he felt the strongest urge to ask why she'd chosen work over watching Ethan this morning. Her choice shouldn't bother him, but it did. Yet he kept silent. They'd shared a delightful evening, and he didn't want to ruin it.

Ellie bathed and dressed Ethan, readying him for bed. Reuben poured them each a glass of iced tea with the hope that she'd stay a few extra minutes after his son was settled in bed.

She arched her eyebrows when she came downstairs and saw the tea. "I'm sorry, but I can't stay. I didn't expect to be this late. My parents will be worried."

He nodded. "I didn't think. I apologize."

"No need," she said with a smile. "I had a nice time." She stepped away from him, left the room for the food pantry and returned within moments with a slice of chocolate cake. "You didn't have dessert."

"Neither did you."

"I know." She set the slice on the kitchen table, then went back to retrieve the entire cake and took out another plate, a knife and two forks. "I can stay a few moments longer for cake."

Reuben chuckled. "I'm glad. Cake and your company—it doesn't get any better than this." And he meant it.

Chapter Fourteen

Ellie was already smitten, but her love for him grew during the evening. The man had been attentive since he'd asked her to supper. The fact that he'd bought the meal, set up the blanket and bought her daisies made him all the more special to her. She cut herself a small piece of cake, then sat down to enjoy the treat with the man seated across from her.

It was as if they were friends who found pleasure in each other's company. Ellie wished they could be more than friends, but she would enjoy whatever time she had left with him—while dreaming of things that could never be.

They ate their cake and drank their tea. When they were finished, Ellie rose and placed the dirty dishes into the wash basin in the sink. She turned on the water and reached below the cabinet for dish detergent, but Reuben stopped her. He came up from behind, gently removed her hand and closed the cabinet door. Then he reached over her shoulder to turn off the water.

"I'll take care of the dishes." His voice rumbled near

her ear, making her tingle where his breath touched her skin.

"I don't mind—"

"This is my night to do something for you. 'Tis the least I can do. You've done so much for me."

He stepped back and she could breathe again, but she was still hyperaware of his scent, his nearness. She turned. "If you're sure…" He nodded, and she said, "I'll go, then."

She grabbed her bag and left the house. Ellie was aware that he followed her closely, escorting her to her vehicle to see her safely inside. It was that time of night when dusk was beginning to settle and darkness was soon to follow.

Ethan was sleeping only a few yards away in the house. Ellie experienced a hitch in her breath as Reuben reached for her hand. She felt the warmth of his fingers against hers as she was assisted inside her buggy.

She felt her face heat as she reached for the leathers and hoped he didn't notice. She breathed evenly, then faced him. "*Danki* again for a lovely night."

"I had a *gut* time."

"Me, too."

"I'll see you tomorrow?"

She inclined her head. "If for some reason I can't make it, I'll make sure Charlie comes in my place." She sensed when he stiffened. "What's wrong?"

He gave her a rueful smile. "Just tired," he said. His smile widened.

"Enjoy the rest of your night."

"The same to you, Ellie Stoltzfus. I'll see you again soon." The way his eyes warmed as he studied her made her feel happy inside.

As she pulled away, she knew she was in deep trouble because she seriously wanted to marry that man. And if she didn't discover a way to change her affections, there was every chance there'd be a broken heart in her future.

For the rest of the week, Ellie babysat for Ethan. Each day, while he was napping, she made phone calls, first to Rebecca to offer her clients, then to help her find someone else to handle the ones the girl couldn't take. Most of her clients were accommodating. They simply wanted someone to clean for them and do a good job. Rebecca took five of her clients, and the rest were divided between others who cleaned house for a living. The Broderick household Ellie kept for now until she could introduce Olivia to Rebecca. She knew the two would get on well.

Since their picnic supper, Reuben had started to come home for lunch. The first time he'd entered the house, she'd gaped at him in shock. She had cooked sliced carrots for Ethan and run them under cold water to cool them down. Ethan was in his high chair, eating the carrots, content with his new food. She'd filled his sippy cup with milk, and he drank from it easily.

Apparently noting her reaction, Reuben apologized for coming unexpectedly.

She scowled at him. "'Tis your *haus*, Reuben. You've a right to come home for lunch."

"The job we started today is just up the road."

"You'll be home for lunch every day, then?"

Reuben hesitated before replying. "*Ja*, if you don't mind."

Her expression softened. "I don't mind."

Reuben continued to come home at noon every day, and Ellie looked forward to his midday visits. She liked figuring out what to make him, and enjoyed his company for the forty-five minutes he had to spend with her.

Friday morning, she was downstairs while Ethan napped in his room when she received a phone call from Olivia Broderick, who pleaded with her to come this afternoon.

"I have company coming, and I need to get the house ready. There's so much to do and I have no energy."

Ellie thought longingly of her anticipated lunch with Reuben. "I can be there at two."

"Thank you, Ellie," Olivia expressed warmly. "You don't know how much this means to me."

After she hung up, Ellie finished cleaning the downstairs, then went into the kitchen to prepare lunch. Ethan would be getting up soon. He'd already outgrown the cradle that Reuben had made for him. She didn't mind going upstairs periodically to check on the little boy. It was easier to get things done around the house when Ethan wasn't sleeping in the great room.

She decided to make BLT sandwiches, but as she looked inside, she saw only two strips of bacon, and she didn't want to give something to Reuben that she wouldn't also be eating. He would be the gentleman and insist that she eat the BLT while he settled for a peanut butter and jelly sandwich. She knew he'd had way too many of those while Sarah was here.

Ellie hadn't had a chance to grocery shop for Reuben. She called her sister Leah, whose craft shop now included a small general store. The building that housed Leah's craft shop had once been a general store owned by her in-laws.

The phone call to Leah at the store went through immediately. When her sister picked up, Ellie explained what she needed. "I know you're busy, but do you think you could find someone to bring them to me? Ethan is napping..."

"I'll bring them," Leah said. "Henry is here, and I could use a break. He'll watch the store for me."

"I don't want to cause you any trouble. I can come after he wakes up." She'd be tight for time if she did that, though—she needed to have lunch ready for Reuben, then she'd head over to the Broderick home after he left. She'd take Ethan to her parents and Charlie could watch him. Then she'd pick him up on her return to the house, and get back before Reuben's arrival in the afternoon. She told Leah of her plan.

"I can stay with Ethan," she offered. "I'm having one of my own. I'd like to spend time with the little one."

"Henry..."

"He won't mind," Leah assured her. Her voice lowered to a whisper. "He loves me."

Ellie smiled. "*Ja*, he does," she said, then paused. "Leah, Reuben will be home for lunch."

There was silence on the other end of the line. "You don't want me there when he comes."

She felt her face heat. "'Tis not that I don't want you here." She drew a calming breath. "Reuben doesn't know I have to work this afternoon."

She could envision her sister's eyes widening. "Why not?"

"Because he wants me to be here, and I will be again...after I finish at the Broderick *haus*."

"He wants you." There was a pregnant pause. "Does he like you?"

Ellie's mind raced to formulate the right words. "I don't know, but he might."

"I think that's *wunderbor*!"

"Please, Leah. You can't tell anyone. Not even Henry." Her stomach burned. "Especially not Meg."

She could sense her sister's disapproval. "I don't keep secrets from my husband, and I don't like keeping them from my sisters."

"'Tis not your secret," she told her. "'Tis mine, and I don't think anything will come of it."

"Fine," Leah said sharply, and Ellie closed her eyes. The last thing she wanted to do was upset her sister.

"I'm sorry."

"No need to apologize." Her sister's tone had softened. "I understand."

Leah told her when she could come, and, relieved, Ellie decided she'd make Reuben custard for dessert since she already had the ingredients on hand. She'd placed the last of the custard cups into the refrigerator when her sister arrived.

Leah looked wonderful, and Ellie told her so. Her sister entered the house with a bag of groceries, and Ellie scolded her for carrying them. "Does Henry allow you to carry in the groceries?"

Leah blushed. "*Nay*. But 'tis only one bag. There are more in the buggy."

Ellie suspected that Henry had wanted to be the one to make the delivery, but Leah had insisted that it be her.

"Please sit down. Would you like tea? I can put the kettle on, then get the rest of the groceries." She hoped that Ethan continued to sleep while she was outside.

She was back in less than a minute with two shopping bags. She paid her sister for the groceries, then put them away. Leah had turned off the stove and was preparing two cups of hot tea. "I see you found the stash of tea."

Leah grinned. "In the pantry, where we keep tea at home."

Ellie nodded. She had done some rearranging in the pantry earlier this week.

The sisters talked about Meg, Charlie and Nell.

"Everyone seems to be doing well. Happy and content in their marriages," Ellie said.

"They are. We all are." Leah eyed her thoughtfully, and Ellie was afraid she'd bring up the subject of Reuben, but she didn't. Ellie offered up a silent prayer of thanks.

Leah glanced at her watch and stood. "I need to get back. Henry will worry, and Reuben will be home soon," she said, adding the last bit with a mischievous smile. "Why don't I stop by Mam and Dat's and ask Charlie to come and watch Ethan for you."

"I don't know if she's free to come."

"I'll call you if she can't make it. If she's busy, you can take him for Mam to watch him. She'd love it."

Ellie worried that she'd be imposing too much on their mother and said so.

"*Nay.* She watched Meg's baby one afternoon before they left for New Wilmington." Leah smiled. "She made out just fine."

Ethan cried out from upstairs.

"Get him. I can see myself out." Her sister grinned at her. "I'll call you to let you know if Charlie can't babysit. If not, maybe you'd like to bring him to the store. 'Tis closer, and Henry and I can both keep an eye on him. It will be on-the-job training for when our baby arrives." She patted her stomach.

"Danki," Ellie murmured.

She went up to get Ethan and smiled when he started babbling when he saw her. She thought she heard him say "da," as if trying to say Dat, but she couldn't be sure. Still, she beamed at him, choosing to believe that he'd called out to his father.

After she changed his diaper, she fed him downstairs. A quick glance at the wall told her it was nearly noon. Reuben would be home any minute. As she sat close to his son, watching him eat, she felt anticipation. She liked spending time with Reuben. She couldn't wait for him to come. With that thought, she rose and grabbed the bacon that Leah had brought for her and what was left in the older package, then she began to make lunch. She fried the bacon until it was crispy but not overdone, then took out the lettuce and tomato and the jar of mayonnaise. She sliced homemade crusty bread, ready to toast on the stove. And she waited for Reuben.

Noon passed, then twelve fifteen. She had to leave after lunch. How late would Reuben be? Finally, she heard his buggy through the open kitchen window. She smiled, pleased, her heart beating with nervous excitement. She turned on the gas, buttered the bread lightly, then set about making toast. Reuben came through the door as she was putting together their BLT sandwiches.

"Ellie," he said warmly. His smile lit up his blue eyes. "Something smells delicious."

"I made BLTs."

His blue eyes brightened. "I love BLTs. I can't remember the last time I had them."

She gestured toward the table. Reuben stopped to ruffle his son's light cap of soft hair. "What would you like to drink?" she asked.

"Is there iced tea left?"

"*Ja*, I made a fresh batch this morning."

"I'll get it," he offered, and he surprised her once again as he took the iced tea pitcher from the refrigerator, then started to reach over her shoulder for two glasses as she turned with plates in hand.

Ellie froze as she found herself face-to-face with Reuben, and so close she could detect his scent combined with soap and water. He must have washed up outside before coming home.

Home. How would it feel if this were her home as Reuben's wife? He hadn't mentioned marriage again. Had he changed his mind? The thought saddened her. But then she recalled the picnic they'd shared at the beginning of the week. He'd been kind, almost romantic. The evening hadn't been arranged by someone who didn't care.

Was he silently courting her? Trying to change her mind? Brightening, she experienced warmth in her heart. There were still problems to work out. He had difficulty accepting help for one, and the other, the big one—he didn't want more children, and Ellie desperately wanted a large family.

She put the sandwiches on the table. Reuben had sat down after fixing each of them a glass of iced tea. It was almost as if they were married. The feel in the kitchen was of a family—father, mother and son—eating together. Only Reuben wasn't her husband, nor Ethan her son. A longing rose up in her that nearly stole her breath.

Reuben narrowed his gaze on her after apparently noting the change. "What's wrong?"

She gave him a genuine smile after fighting back the myriad emotions she felt. "I'm worried about my parents," she said, because it was another obstacle in her marrying.

"Are they ill?" he asked with concern.

"*Nay*, but I can see them aging. Mam needs my help in the kitchen and with doing chores." She looked down at her plate, unwilling to be drawn deeper into her attraction toward him. "Dat is doing well enough, but he still worries me."

"Why?" Reuben's voice was soft.

She glanced up at him briefly. "I don't know. 'Tis something that I feel."

He was silent, but she could feel his gaze. She transferred her attention to Ethan, smiling as she gave him another carrot slice and watched as he bit into it.

"Ellie."

She locked gazes with him. *"Ja?"*

He shook his head. "Never mind."

She frowned. "What is it?"

"I think you may be worrying more than you should. 'Tis *gut* that you want to help your parents. I'm glad of that." His voice became husky. "I'm grateful you've given up time with them to be here. For Ethan." He paused. "And for me."

Ellie blinked. She couldn't let him see what was in her heart, especially if he was no longer interested in marriage. But he wasn't looking at her like she was just a friend. She was confused. She knew what she wanted to do, but she was worried her choice would lead her down a spiraling path to heartbreak and unhappiness.

Not that Reuben wasn't an honorable man. She was sure if she married him he would treat her right.

She pushed everything out of her mind. She was here with Reuben, and she needed to enjoy his company before Sarah came back. She looked at his plate and smiled at him. "You liked your BLT?"

He nodded, his smile a little slower in forming. "Delicious."

"Do you want another one?"

Reuben shook his head as he stood. "'Tis getting late. I need to get back to work."

Ellie watched as he bent to place a gentle kiss on his son's forehead. Her heart melted. He loved his son. Now if only he would love her.

She watched as he grabbed his hat from a wall peg before he headed toward the door. After a quick glance at Ethan to ensure he was fine, she followed him to the door and outside. He started toward his vehicle. Suddenly, he halted and faced her.

"I hope you're still thinking about my marriage proposal," he said.

Ellie drew in a sharp breath as she nodded.

His face lit up as he spun back to continue to his buggy. He climbed in and steered the horse back to the road, then glanced at her and waved as he continued on. Ellie felt breathless and excited and worried and scared as she reentered the house.

Ethan babbled to her, and she lifted him from his chair and hugged him. "I'd love to be your *mam*, little man, but I don't know if I can. While I love you—and your *vadder*—I want you to have brothers and sisters. But your *dat* wants you to be an only child."

A quick glance at her watch had her gasping with

stunned disbelief. She hadn't heard from Leah so Charlie must be on her way. She needed to gather her cleaning supplies and get ready for her arrival. She had a cleaning job to do for a sick client, and she didn't want to upset her by being late.

The image of Reuben's expression after she confessed with a simple nod that she was still considering his proposal warmed her from the inside out. How she loved that man and his little boy! Yet that didn't mean she'd settle for less than she wanted, needed. She'd have to come to a decision soon, and she feared either choice would be a difficult road to travel.

Chapter Fifteen

Reuben finished his workday and was eager to get home. To Ellie. The fact that she acknowledged that she was considering his marriage proposal gave him hope. He loved her. He never thought he'd fall this hard and quickly in love with anyone, but he had with her. He knew there were problems to overcome, solutions to discuss. She wanted another child. Could he go through the worry and fear again while waiting for her to give birth?

He would. For Ellie. He loved her too much not to give her what she wanted. And the thought of their tiny baby in his arms brought him joy. As long as nothing went wrong during the baby's birth or shortly afterward—he couldn't imagine raising two children on his own. If something happened to Ellie, he'd never marry again. Even to have a mother for his children. He'd just have to rely more on help from the community. *Accepting help.* Something else he had to work on.

The more he thought about his life with Ellie, the more he wanted it. He would give her children. He would love them and Ellie. But he knew she had concerns—his Ellie. He just had to convince her that it would be all right.

He pulled into his driveway and up to the house. He hurried inside, eager to see her, talk with her and confess his change of heart. Would she believe him? Would she look at him with joy? He caught his breath as he secured his horse and approached the house. Would she gaze at him with love?

What if she didn't love him? He realized then that he wouldn't marry her if she didn't. As he reached for the door, he offered a silent prayer to the Lord. *Please, Lord, let Ellie love me. I want to marry her and I need Your blessing. And Your guidance to do the right thing when the time comes.*

He stepped inside the house, his gaze searching. He heard sounds from the great room and went inside. But he didn't see the blond-haired woman he loved. He found someone else instead—her red-haired sister. He experienced a burning in his belly as he studied Charlie, who was changing his son's diaper.

"Charlie," he said.

Her gaze rose as she regarded him with a smile. "You're home! *Gut.*" She lifted the soiled diaper and set it in the diaper pail. Then she turned to face him.

"Where's Ellie?"

"She had to houseclean for a client, so she asked me to watch Ethan."

Reuben nodded, keeping his expression polite, but inside he was struggling to understand why Ellie had left again. Because she couldn't bear to face him after their parting words?

Charlie, unaware of his turmoil, picked up Ethan, then handed his son to him. "I think he misses his *vadder.*

Ellie heard it and so did I—your *soohn* was calling you today. We're sure we heard him say *Dat*." She grinned. "See? Even while you're at work, he thinks of you."

He held Ethan close to his chest, studying Charlie as she got ready to leave. "Will Ellie be back tomorrow?" he asked casually, attempting to hide his feelings.

"I'm sure she will. What time do you need her?"

"Does she need to help your *mudder*?"

Charlie shrugged. "She likes to help her, but I doubt she'll need to tomorrow. I'll be there, and my sisters are coming. We'll be cooking food together for Sunday."

"I'll see her tomorrow, then. She can come when she likes. I have a few things I need to fix around the house, and I'd appreciate it if she'd watch Ethan while I work."

Charlie studied him thoughtfully. "I'll tell her," she said. Then she left.

Reuben couldn't help wondering if Ellie was avoiding him again, even though he thought their lunches together had gone well. Every moment they'd spent together had been good.

He would ask her tomorrow for the truth. If Ellie sent someone in her place, then he'd know what her decision was.

"Da. Da. Da." Ethan patted his cheek and repeated his sounds.

He gazed at his son, saw that Ethan had his eyes on him as he continued to say, "Da. Da. Dat." He distinctly heard the *t* on that last word. He grinned. His baby had just spoken his name.

The next day he got up early, showered and dressed. Would Ellie come at the regular time? Or send someone else?

He hoped not. He wanted her to come, but more than that, he wanted to spend time with her.

Shortly afterward, after he'd taken Ethan from his crib, then gone downstairs ready for the day, Reuben heard the sound of buggy wheels. He resisted the urge to peer out the window. If it was Charlie instead of Ellie, he'd find out soon enough. He heard the door-knob rattle, then turn.

Ellie entered the house with her head down, unaware that he sat at the table watching her.

She was lovely in a bright purple dress with white apron and prayer *kapp*, her blond hair golden. He realized that she was struggling to carry in two huge bags. He immediately went to her.

"Ellie, let me help you."

She gasped and jolted. "Reuben, I didn't see you."

He regarded her with amusement. "You were busy trying to carry too much at one time." He tugged on one bag, and she released it into his care. He lifted it to test its weight. "What do you have in here?"

She blushed, avoided his glance. "Just a few things."

He stared at her. "What things?"

"I cooked last night. I brought food to share." Her gaze met his, then skittered away. "And I stopped for a few groceries."

Her thoughtfulness made him feel warm inside. "Picnic food?" he teased.

She carried the other bag and lifted it onto the kitchen counter. "That depends," she murmured, "on what you consider picnic food."

Reuben carried the other bag and placed it next to the one she'd set down. "Picnic food is anything we can eat outside."

Ellie turned then, and he felt the impact of her beautiful blue eyes. "Then I guess we have picnic food." She bit her lip. "You're not angry?"

Reuben stilled. "Because you shopped for me?"

She bobbed her head.

"I want to pay you for the food."

"You may pay me for the few groceries but not what I cooked."

"Oll recht," he said agreeably. She was wonderful. It took all he had not to ask her again to marry him. He wanted, needed an answer. He stood for several minutes, watching her put away the food. He could sense that she was growing tense. He frowned.

She shot him a glance. "Don't you have work to do?"

"Ja, I thought I'd install new flooring in the bedrooms upstairs."

She arched an eyebrow. "All of them?"

"I'll start with the largest room, then go from there."

"Did you eat breakfast?" she asked.

He nodded. "I ate a bowl of cereal."

"I'll fix you lunch when you want it. Just let me know." She bent to kiss Ethan's smooth baby cheek.

Seeing them together reminded him of Ethan's recent words. "He said *Dat,*" Reuben said with a wide smile. "He said *Da-da* first, but then I heard the *t* sound at the end of the last one. He said *Dat.* He said my name."

Ellie regarded his son with a softness that Reuben yearned to have aimed at him. As if she'd heard his inner thoughts, she met his gaze, her eyes crinkling with enjoyment, her lips curving into a soft smile. "Congratulations, Dat. Your son recognizes how special you are to him."

Am I special to you?

"Go to work. Ethan and I will be fine." She went to the refrigerator for a cup with two handles containing milk.

"I didn't know he could drink out of that." His lips twisted. "He's growing fast."

Ellie nodded. "Now will you go to work?"

"Are you trying to get rid of me?"

She blushed but didn't say anything. Why? Because it was the truth?

"I'll be upstairs in the master bedroom," he said gruffly, then he left her before he said something he didn't mean. She hadn't stayed yesterday afternoon because she'd worked. He wanted to ask her why the sudden need to houseclean. But he didn't. He didn't want to be at odds with her. It was all right to have disagreements, but he didn't want them while he waited for Ellie's decision about marriage. Until then, he'd try to woo her so she'd realize how deep his feelings were for her. And hope that she'd begin to feel the same way.

He had brought up the flooring yesterday after Charlie had left and Ethan was in bed for the night. He went upstairs and got to work. And tried not to wonder why Ellie had found it more important to houseclean for somebody than spend time with Ethan. *And me.*

Ellie frowned as she watched Ethan eat his breakfast. She had put away the food she'd brought and made herself a cup of tea, then grabbed a fresh muffin before she sat next to her charge.

"Da-dat!" Ethan said.

She grinned. "*Gut* boy!" She broke off a piece of sweet muffin and placed it on his tray. He'd already eaten his cereal. She eyed him fondly as he picked up the broken-off bit and put it in his mouth. As he chewed, his eyes got big. Ethan loved the new food.

She wasn't sure what to do while Reuben was upstairs working. There was a new added tension between them. She urged him to work because she'd needed some space. He'd reminded her of his marriage proposal. She wasn't sure what to do. She loved him, but should she marry him? There was still so much between them—the memory of his late wife, his avowal that he would marry only for Ethan, her parents' well-being. She no longer worried about her business, having decided that she'd had enough. And then there was Meg. The fact that he and her sister had once had a relationship, if a short one. Would Meg be upset if she accepted Reuben's marriage proposal?

There was only one way to find out. She'd visit Meg and ask.

There was also the fact that Reuben didn't accept help well. Her family would want to be there for her new family. They would want to pitch in whenever there was a construction project or if they needed someone to watch their children.

Ellie closed her eyes and had a mental image of what it might be like to marry Reuben. It would be wonderful if he loved her. She could see herself large with child, Reuben's concern as the midwife arrived to deliver their baby. He would look anguished but he would kiss her, tell her he loved her, and he would wait downstairs with her father and other family members while her baby was born. It would be hard giving birth, but Ellie could see her joy after the midwife placed a little girl into her arms. No, wait! There was another one—a baby boy. Twins!

She gasped and opened her eyes. Why on earth did she envision twins? Because it would mean less stress if Reuben had to worry through only one pregnancy and birth?

She loved him. She wanted a life with him, but she couldn't decide what to do.

Ellie took Ethan outside after breakfast. It was warm, but it was still early enough to enjoy the day. She studied the backyard. Green filled the empty spaces left by the rusted junk after it was removed. Reuben had put up a clothesline, and Ellie decided that she'd do the wash later in the afternoon. *Just like a wife,* she thought.

She took Ethan for a walk about the property. Carrying him on her left hip, she showed him a honeysuckle bush with its rich fragrance, keeping him far enough away so the bees wouldn't bother them. It was quiet, peaceful. A good day to think about the future. To silently pray to God.

The morning flew by as she explored the grounds with Ethan. She glanced at her wristwatch and gasped. It was nearly noon. She had been teaching Ethan to walk by holding on to his hands, a great way to strengthen his legs for when he could walk by himself.

As she entered the kitchen, she saw that Reuben had come downstairs. He seemed harried, upset. It looked as if he'd run his hand through his hair, for it was tousled.

"Where were you?" he asked sharply.

Ellie stiffened, not liking his tone. "We were outside, enjoying the day."

"You could have told me." The tension had left his frame.

"I didn't want to disturb you." She looked away and carried Ethan to his high chair. He had missed his morning nap. He was sleepy. Ellie debated whether to feed him or put him to bed. "Is Ethan's room done?" She met his gaze.

"*Nay*, but the other rooms are."

She nodded. "After lunch, I thought I would take Ethan to my parents' for a nap."

Reuben narrowed his gaze. "He can sleep here."

"Actually, he can't. He doesn't sleep well with noise anymore." She went to the refrigerator and took out a piece of American cheese, then broke it into pieces, which she set on the little boy's plate. "Do you want lunch? I brought cold roast beef. I can make you a sandwich."

He was silent, so Ellie turned. There was an odd look in his expression, which he quickly masked when he caught her gaze. "I could eat."

She nodded, then prepared lunch for the three of them. She made sandwiches for her and Reuben after asking if he wanted mayonnaise on his. She took potato salad and pickles out of the refrigerator and set them on the table, poured them each a glass of iced tea and gave Ethan a serving of cooked cold peas.

As the three of them ate their lunch, Ellie thought it felt as if they were a family. Reuben had let go of his sour mood. He ate with enjoyment, praising her for the food, thanking her again for caring for Ethan.

"I don't mind if you want to take Ethan to your parents' *haus*."

Ellie was surprised at his change of heart. "We don't have to go. I just thought it would be quieter there for his nap."

"*Ja*," he agreed. "By the time you get home, I'll have

finished the flooring." He hesitated. "What time do you think you'll be back?"

She thought of Ethan's usual nap time and factored in that Reuben's son had forgone his morning sleep. "Three thirty? He didn't nap this morning so I don't know how long he'll sleep."

"Three thirty is fine." But there was something in his gaze that made her wonder if, despite his agreement, he was disappointed that she and Ethan were leaving.

"If he wakes up sooner, I'll bring him home," she said.

His expression warmed. "That would be *gut. Danki.*"

After she cleaned up, she and Ethan left while Reuben went back to work. The thought occurred to visit Meg before heading to her parents'. Peter and Meg's house was a little out of the way, but not by much. Her belly burned and she was nervous. How would Meg react to Reuben's proposal to her?

She turned onto the dirt drive leading to the house. Her heart started to hammer hard. This was her sister. How could she consider marrying Reuben if Meg had a problem with it? And that was assuming she knew that she wanted to marry Reuben, despite the problems that seemed insurmountable between them.

Her breath hitched as, with Ethan in her arms, she climbed Meg's front porch. She lifted a hand to knock but the door swung open, revealing her sister, who grinned at her. Then her blue eyes dropped to the child in her arms and her expression changed.

Chapter Sixteen

"Ellie!" Meg exclaimed, her gaze shifting from her to Ethan. "Come in!" With her young son on her hip, she stepped aside to allow them entry.

"How was your trip to New Wilmington? Was his family there nice?"

"I had a great time. Everyone fussed over Timothy."

"*Gut, gut,* then you enjoyed yourself."

Meg nodded.

"We're on our way to our *eldre,*" Ellie said. "I thought I'd stop by and maybe have a cup of hot tea with you."

"Sounds *wunderbor.* Timothy just got up from his nap."

Ellie frowned. "I can't stay long. Ethan hasn't slept yet." She sensed her sister's curiosity as she followed Meg down the hall to the kitchen in the back of the house.

Meg went right to the stove and put the kettle on. There was a high chair in the corner of the room. Ellie's nephew was too young to sit in it yet, but it was there for when he got just a little bit older. Her sister set her son into the baby seat that sat on the table. "Watch him for me?"

She nodded, and Meg pulled over the high chair. "I could have done that."

"I'm not helpless."

"I know," Ellie said as she placed Ethan in the chair.

The kettle whistled, and Meg fixed two cups of tea, then handed one to Ellie. Her sister sat across from her. "Something's bothering you."

Ellie inhaled sharply but nodded.

"Does it have something to do with this little one?" Meg asked softly. "Who is he?" She narrowed her gaze. "He looks familiar."

"His name is Ethan Miller. He's Reuben's son." She saw her sister's mouth drop open. "I've been watching him for nearly three weeks now." She bit her lip. "Reuben's a widower. He recently moved into our church district."

Meg didn't say anything at first. Ellie felt her chest tighten.

"That's why he looks familiar. Ethan looks like his *vadder*."

Ellie nodded. "Meg... I wanted—needed—to talk with you." She explained how she came to be cleaning house for Reuben, who hadn't wanted her there at first. About his grief over the death of his wife. "I became friends with Sarah, his sister, who was babysitting for him until he could marry or hire someone else to watch Ethan..."

She noted the changing expressions on Meg's face before she continued. "Reuben's *mudder* got hurt and their parents needed Sarah. Sarah asked me to take care of Ethan until her return, but that was weeks ago and she's still not ready to come back."

"How did you manage Ethan with your housecleaning business?"

"At first, Charlie watched him in the mornings for me, and I took over in the afternoons. Now I take care of Ethan full-time."

"So what's the problem?"

"I'm in love with Reuben." She saw the startled look on Meg's face. "And he asked me to marry him, but I haven't given him my answer yet."

"I don't understand. If you love him, why won't you marry him?"

Ellie felt her throat tighten. She blinked back tears. "He wants to marry so his son will have a *mudder*. He doesn't want love. He said he'd already loved and lost and won't go through the pain again."

"*Ach nay*, Ellie!" her sister said quietly. "What are you going to do?"

"The idea of me with Reuben doesn't bother you?"

"Why should it? I have a husband whom I love with all my heart. I was infatuated with Reuben years ago, but once I was with him, there was nothing there. My heart always belonged to Peter. Reuben with you or anyone else won't affect me one way or another."

"But if I marry him, he'll become part of the family."

Meg smiled. "As would this precious young man here." She locked gazes with Ellie. "You love Ethan, too."

Ellie nodded. "*Ja*, I adore him. He's so smart. Do you know he said *Dat*? Reuben was thrilled."

"You will marry Reuben, then?"

"I don't know," she whispered. "Meg, he thinks Ethan is enough. He doesn't want more children."

Her sister's features softened with compassion. "And you've always wanted a large family."

"Ja." She turned to Ethan, ran a finger gently down his arm, enjoying the smoothness of his baby skin. "You know Reuben better than anyone. What should I do?"

"I don't know him as well as you do. He took me home a couple of times from singing and once we went on an outing with Peter and…" She smiled ruefully, shook her head. "Then the accident happened, and Peter and I were asked to plan a Christmas birthday celebration for his mother and our *dat,* and everything changed." Meg reached across the table and placed a hand over Ellie's. "You have to decide what means more to you…being Reuben's wife or a mother of a large family."

"But there's more. I'm worried about Mam and Dat. If I marry, then how will I help with the chores? I've caught Mam struggling with a heavy pan, and Dat needs help with the animals. I don't know what to do!"

"Ellie, our parents have three daughters who are married to strong, healthy men. And Charlie's Nate is always willing to lend a helping hand. What makes our parents your responsibility alone?"

"I don't know. I've just felt that way."

"Well, stop it. Mam and Dat will be upset to know that you've felt this way. They have all of us to help them. Don't make them an excuse for not marrying Reuben. If you love him, marry him. You need to decide one way or another."

"I know." Ellie noted that Ethan was nearly asleep in his chair. She stood. She had a lot to think about. "I should get to the *haus*. This little boy desperately needs a nap." She moved to unstrap him from the chair. "Meg, if Peter hadn't wanted children, would you still have married him?"

Meg frowned. "*Ja*, because I loved him too much to live without him."

Pressing Ethan's head against her shoulder, Ellie exchanged smiles with her sister. "You'd be *oll recht* with it if I say *ja* to Reuben?"

"As long as you're happy, I'm fine with it."

"*Danki*, Meg. For the talk and the tea."

Meg stood at the door while Ellie set Ethan in his buggy seat. The child woke up crying and out of sorts. "Don't fret, my little man. You'll be cozy and asleep once we get to Mam's."

Ellie put Ethan to bed at her parents'. He fell into a deep sleep immediately, and she went downstairs to see what she could do for her mother.

The rain started midday. It continued as a heavy downpour that seemed like it wouldn't stop anytime soon. Ellie was due to bring Ethan home at three thirty, but because of her stop at Meg's, Ethan hadn't gone down for his nap until late. After missing his morning sleep, the little boy would probably be out for more than two hours yet. At three fifteen, Ellie decided to drive to Reuben's to explain the situation. Her mother agreed to keep an eye and ear out for Ethan sound asleep in her room. Ellie prayed that Reuben wouldn't be mad at her.

Reuben finished the floor in less time than he'd expected. In an hour or so, they would be able to walk on the floor, and next time Ethan wouldn't have to go to the Arlin Stoltzfus's *haus* for a nap. And Ellie would be here. He made his lunch at noon, then went back to work. Once he'd finished the two rooms, he cleaned up downstairs and took a seat at the kitchen table. The house seemed empty without Ethan. *Without Ellie.* What if she didn't want to marry him?

It was getting late. Past three thirty. Maybe Ethan was sleeping late and she didn't want to wake him. But she knew he expected her home at three thirty. He began to pace. It had started to rain. As the clock struck four, he became afraid. The rain was a heavy downpour, and the memory of his buggy accident late at night during a rainstorm made him uneasy. Should he drive over to the Stoltzfuses'? See that they were still there and all right?

The rain beat hard against the roof. Reuben peered out the kitchen window, saw water pooling on the driveway and on the lawn, running off the roof of the old barn. A crack of thunder startled him, and he decided at that moment that he couldn't stay any longer. He left his hat and ran to his buggy, silently apologizing to the animal for the rain. He drove onto the road after twice checking both ways for traffic. The last thing he needed was for a car to zoom up behind him and drive him off the road.

His hands were shaking as he held the reins and spurred the horse into a fast trot. *Please, Lord, keep them safe.* He was scared. This day reminded him of another. He had a baby son he loved…and the woman of his heart whom he loved and wanted to marry.

The rain was blinding, and he had to slow the horse down. Just a little farther, then he'd be at his destination. And that's when he saw a buggy off to the side of the road, close to a pond on the far side of an English farmer's property.

Nay! He pulled his buggy over and ran toward the vehicle. It was on its side, leaning toward the water. *Ethan! Ellie! Lord, please let them be all right!*

There was no one inside the vehicle. He saw the wooden child's buggy seat. It had tipped over inside. "Ellie! Ethan!"

He heard a soft moan. He skirted the front of the buggy and saw her lying on her back in the water. He could see a small cut on her forehead. He stared, knowing that he would have to go into the pond to get her. "*Gott*, please help me," he murmured over and over like a litany of prayer.

Ellie's life and perhaps that of his son relied on his getting to the woman he loved as quickly as possible. He knew how to swim. It wasn't like the last time. He'd taken swimming lessons, for he never wanted to feel helpless near the water again. He stepped in, lowered his body into the water and did the breaststroke until he reached Ellie's side.

Reuben offered up a silent prayer of thanks when he reached her.

"Ellie."

She opened her eyes. "Reuben?"

"*Ja*, dear one, 'tis me." He surrounded her with his arms and started toward the shore.

"I'm sorry."

His pulse raced with fear. "Are you *oll recht*?" He saw her nod. "Where's Ethan?"

"Safe. He's with Mam. I didn't want to be late… needed to tell you why. Late to nap. I'm sorry."

Near the shoreline, he picked her up in his arms and cradled her against him. "Nothing to be sorry for, El.

'Tis me who's sorry. I love you. I should have told you sooner."

But Ellie's eyes had closed. Alarm tensed up his body. "Ellie?"

She drew and exhaled a sharp breath. "I'm fine."

"You need a hospital."

"*Nay.* Take me back to Mam and Dat's. Please?"

He couldn't deny her anything. He set her gently in his buggy. He would see to her safety and have someone fetch her vehicle. He retrieved her horse and tied him to the back of his buggy.

The downpour had eased as he climbed in and drove down the road, moving slowly to protect the horse tied up behind his vehicle. Ellie sat next to him. She leaned against the back of the seat with her eyes closed.

"Ellie," he said urgently. "Dear one, open your eyes. Let me know how you feel."

Her eyes flickered open. "Reuben?"

"*Ja*, Ellie. 'Tis me." He regarded her with concern. "You're almost home. Do you hurt anywhere?"

"My head a little, but I'll be fine."

"Are you certain? We can call the ambulance."

"*Nay*, Reuben. I just want to go home."

"Almost there."

He carried Ellie as he climbed the steps and knocked hard. Twice. The door swung open, revealing Missy, who cried out when she saw Ellie in his arms. "Is there someplace I can put her? She said her head hurts, but otherwise I don't think she's seriously injured. I still think she should see a doctor, though." He laid her gently on the sofa, grabbing a pillow from a chair and placing it carefully under her head.

"What happened?" Missy cried as Arlin entered the

room. Ellie's father took one look at his daughter on the sofa and turned pale.

"I was worried when she didn't come back. I started over here to make sure they were safe. I found her in Prescott's pond. She was floating on her back. I was able to get to her and bring her to shore. Your horse is tied to the back of my buggy." He hesitated. "I drove slowly."

Missy regarded him with tears in her eyes. "*Danki*, Reuben."

"Don't thank me. She must have been on her way to see me. I know she was worried about bringing Ethan home late. 'Tis my fault that she had the accident."

Arlin stepped up close to him. "Now see here, Reuben Miller, you are not responsible for this accident. It was Ellie's idea to go out in the rain in the first place. Don't you beat yourself up over this, do you hear?"

Taken aback by her father's tirade, Reuben could only nod. "You've all done so much for me. I can't put into words how grateful I am."

The man flicked his hand in the air, dismissing his gratitude. "You saved my daughter. I'll never be able to thank you enough."

Reuben felt the warmth and love of this family as it surrounded him. His eyes stung and he blinked. "Ethan sleeping?"

Missy nodded. "He was extra tired. Ellie felt bad that she didn't get him down for a nap earlier."

He regarded Ellie's mother with a soft expression. "Ellie has nothing to feel bad about. She's been *wunderbor*. I don't know how I'd have gotten along without her." *In fact, I love her.*

"Arlin," he said to her father. "May I have a word with you?" He hesitated. "Alone."

The man nodded. "We can talk in the kitchen. Charlie's at Nell's. 'Tis just us here."

Reuben gave one last look of longing toward Ellie where she rested on the sofa, eyes closed. "Is it *oll recht* to leave her?"

"*Ja*, her mother will stay with her."

She was soaked through, but her parents hadn't hesitated at having her on their furniture. "Thank the Lord that it's not winter," he murmured.

"Amen," Arlin whispered.

The two men entered the kitchen and sat down across the table from each other.

"What's on your mind, Reuben?"

"Ellie."

"What about her?"

"I'd like permission to marry your daughter if she'll have me." He felt his face heat as he looked away briefly. "I asked her, but she's not made up her mind. If she won't have me, I'll understand and leave her in peace. But if there is a chance she wants to be my wife, then I'd like to know that I have your blessing."

Arlin frowned. "You came to me instead of the bishop?"

Reuben nodded. "*Ja*, I know 'tis unusual, but after what just happened, I felt I had to confess how I feel. I love her. I know 'tis only been nine months since Susanna died, but Ellie…she makes me feel alive. She's strong and wise, and I've never met a more generous and loving woman. I desperately want her to be my wife."

Ellie's father eyed Reuben thoughtfully, as if to gauge his measure. "She may not have you."

He experienced pain in the middle of his chest. "I know."

"But then again, she may be stubborn and strong enough to take you on."

Reuben looked at the man with hope. "Arlin?"

"If my daughter wants to marry you, then you have my blessing. But there are things that need saying between you two, I imagine, since she hasn't made a decision yet."

"There are," he agreed.

Missy entered the room and went to the cabinet to take down a box of what Reuben recognized as headache powder. Grabbing a glass from a different cabinet, she filled it with water, then disappeared into the next room.

"Do you think she needs a doctor?"

"I don't know." Arlin looked worried. "I've had worries over Meg, but this one rarely gets sick or hurt."

"I'm responsible for your worries," Reuben admitted. "Over Meg."

"Nonsense, *soohn*. We've never for one moment cast blame on you. It was an accident, nothing more, and by the grace of the Lord, all came out well."

"Still... I didn't know how to swim then. If Peter hadn't stopped..."

"But he did, so don't fret over it. I don't, and after I heard what you told Missy, you must have learned to swim since then."

Reuben nodded. "I'm so thankful that I did...or I wouldn't have been able to pull Ellie from the water."

Arlin regarded him with respect. "I think you'll make a *gut soohn* if the girl will have you. We already love your little one."

He smiled. "He's a *gut* boy. Do you know that he says *Dat* now?"

The older man laughed. "Does he, now? 'tis a thrill, isn't it?"

"*Ja!* Ellie told me he said it, and now that I've heard it for myself…"

"You enjoy being a *vadder*."

"I do." But he'd lost his wife to childbirth. "I'd have liked to have more, but my wife…she died within minutes after giving Ethan life."

"The Lord must have been ready to welcome her home."

"*Ja*, but…" He thought of Ellie. He didn't want anything bad to happen to her, yet, she'd had an accident. He couldn't protect her from life. She wanted children. He wanted more children. It would be worrisome and scary, but he wanted Ellie as his wife and the mother of his children. More than anything, he realized. If he told her, would she believe him?

"I have to confess," he told Arlin, "that I thought to marry only for Ethan's sake. I wasn't looking for love. I was grieving for my wife, and I couldn't bear the thought of falling in love again only to lose the woman I love."

"You're afraid something will happen to my *dochter* like it did to your Susanna."

Reuben nodded. *"Ja."*

"You can't stop life and the will of the Father, Reuben. If 'tis one thing I've learned, it is that things both *gut* and bad happen to families, to people. You have to accept the bad with the *gut* and enjoy every moment of this precious life that God has given us."

"I know that now. I understand."

"Well, then what are you waiting for? Go see the woman you love and get her to agree to marry you."

"*Danki*, Arlin."

"What for?"

"For giving me a wonderful example of a *gut vadder.*"

To his surprise, Arlin looked embarrassed.

Reuben pushed back his chair, then after a nod in his prospective father-in-law's direction, he went to see if his girl—the woman he loved—would have him.

Her head hurt. She couldn't believe she'd lost control of her vehicle. It had been pouring heavily and difficult to see. When the dog ran across the road, she'd tried to steer her horse to avoid him. The next thing she knew, she had run off the road and her buggy had tipped to the side after throwing her outside it. She'd landed with a splash in the pond. She knew how to swim, but her head hurt and it took all she had just to turn to float on her back until someone stopped to help.

Reuben. It had been Reuben who'd pulled her from the water, murmuring gently all the way, picking her up as if she were precious cargo and settling her gently inside his buggy.

Her mother had brought her something for her headache. The powder wasn't a favorite of hers. It tasted nasty, and she had to quickly swallow a full glass of water to chase it down.

She was sore, but except for a slight headache, she wasn't hurt. Reuben had been so kind and caring. Did he love her? Had she been worrying over nothing?

The man in her thoughts entered the great room and moved to her side. She saw her mother exchange looks with him before Mam excused herself and left the room, leaving the two of them alone.

"How are you feeling?" he said huskily.

"My head aches, but I'm fine. I took something for the pain. I'm sure I'll be right as rain in the morning." She laughed at the mention of rain before the memory of the moments before the accident sobered her.

Reuben pulled a chair up close to the sofa where she lay. "Ellie, I have to tell you something, but I don't think you'll believe me…and I'm not telling you now because of your accident. I've been trying to come up with a *gut* time to say what's on my mind."

Ellie eyed him warily. Was he going to admit that he'd proposed for all the wrong reasons? And just when she'd decided to say yes?

"Ellie. Elizabeth Stoltzfus, I've asked you to marry me and you've been thinking about it. I gave you the wrong idea about my reasons—"

"Reuben, you don't have to tell me. I understand that you've changed your mind."

"Changed my—*nay*! I haven't changed my mind or my feelings for you. Ellie, I love you. I want to marry you because you're everything I've ever wanted as my partner in life. I've tried to give you time, but I…in this, the accident might have something to do with it… I can't wait anymore. If you don't want to marry me, please just say so. If you do, you'll make me the happiest man alive."

Ellie couldn't believe what she was hearing. "But there are things we don't agree on…such as children."

"I want children with you. I've realized that I can't stop bad things happening in my life, but I can enjoy the *gut*. And Ellie, you are all that's *gut* and wonderful to me. I love you. I want you to be my wife. Will you marry me?"

She studied him with affection. "You're going to let my family help you when we need it?"

Reuben nodded. "*Ja.* And I'm eager to lend a helping hand back."

"And you think you can put up with me for the rest of your life? I can be challenging."

"I can. I want to." He eyed her with hope.

"*Ja.*"

He blinked. "Are you saying—?"

"*Ja*, I will marry you and be your wife. I will be a *mam* to Ethan and any future children we may have." She touched his cheek above his beard. "And I'll love you forever."

She was shocked to see tears fill her beloved's eyes. "Ellie," he whispered. He bent close and kissed her softly on the lips. She loved being close to him. She was blushing when he lifted his head. "I love you, Ellie."

"I believe you. And I love you." She smiled. "I guess you won't be needing Sarah to return. Except for our wedding."

"When will you marry me?" he asked.

"I have an idea, but I'll have to talk with my sister first. Would you mind marrying in a double ceremony with Charlie and Nate?"

"This November?"

"*Ja.*"

"I'm a widower. We don't have to wait until November. 'Tis only the end of August."

"We can talk about this later," she suggested. "When I'm feeling better?"

"Now that you agreed, I'm eager to make you mine."

Maybe they could marry in September, she thought. She'd suggest it later. "I am yours, Reuben Miller."

"Praise the Lord," Reuben murmured.

Her parents entered the room. Ellie saw her father and husband-to-be exchange glances. Reuben gave a little nod. Her *dat* grinned.

"I take it that little boy asleep in your room is soon to be my grandson?"

"Do you mind?" Ellie asked, pleased at the ease between her parents and future spouse.

"I'm always happy to welcome new members of our family."

They heard a sound from upstairs. "Ethan," Ellie murmured, starting to rise.

"*Nay*. Stay where you are. I'll get him," her mother offered. "I imagine he's hungry. You're staying for supper, Reuben, *ja*?"

"I will, *danki*."

Ellie locked gazes with her husband-to-be, and they shared a secret smile. "Go get our precious boy, Mam."

Epilogue

A year later

Ellie breathed through the contraction, then sighed with relief as it eased. The pains were coming more frequently now. Childbirth hurt, but she was fine. She was strong and she could do this. She couldn't wait to hold the baby—hers and Reuben's—and to calm her worried husband.

"You're doing fine, Ellie," the midwife said.

"Is my husband downstairs? I want to see him."

"He is, but I don't think it's a *gut* idea to have him come in."

"Please? Just for a moment."

"Just for a moment, then."

The midwife left and Ellie was overcome with another sharp contraction. She breathed through the pain, and once again it dissipated. Soon, there would be no relief as her labor progressed.

Reuben burst into the room, looking anxious. He leaned in close. "What's wrong? Are you *oll recht*?"

Ellie smiled and waved him closer. "I just have a

moment but I wanted—needed—to tell you that I love you, and I'll be fine."

"I love you, Ellie." There were tears in his eyes.

She reached up to caress his cheek. "I love you. Now stop worrying and go back downstairs. Mary will come get you as soon as our baby is born."

He left but only after glancing back over his shoulder at her several times. And not a moment too soon. Her contractions began in earnest. Less than an hour later, she gave birth to a beautiful baby girl. She smiled at the midwife, then gasped as she felt another sharp pain in her abdomen. "What's wrong?" she asked Mary. If something happened to her, Reuben would take the blame and never forgive himself.

"This is a surprise, Ellie. Looks like you're having twins, as there is another baby about to make an appearance. Your baby is in the right position. Go ahead and push."

Three pushes later and out came a baby boy. "You have fraternal twins!" Mary said with a grin. She opened the door. "Missy, can you come in here?"

"What's wrong?" her mother asked.

Ellie smiled at her mom. "Nothing. But we need your help."

Mam looked confused until Mary handed her Ellie's daughter. "Your *dochter* has given birth to twins."

"Twins!" Missy smiled. "Our family's been doubly blessed."

Mary cleaned and wrapped up the babies, then placed one in each of Ellie's arms. Mary and her mother left the room.

A few minutes later, Reuben entered, looking anxious.

"Hallo, vadder," Ellie said. She had a tiny baby cradled in each arm. He blinked, then gazed at her with wonder. "Come say *hallo* to our babies."

"Twins," he breathed. His blue eyes filled with love and happy tears. "You're well?"

"I'm fine." She smiled. "Never better."

"Praise be to *Gott*!" He placed a gentle kiss first on his wife's forehead, then on his babies. "I love you," he whispered. "So much."

"I love you, husband. Forever. I hope you're ready for a busy life."

"Absolutely."

Ellie laughed. "You sound so sure."

"I am." He grinned before he bent to kiss her. "Time to share our babies with the rest of our family." He gazed at her sharply to make sure she was ready for visitors. "A short visit only."

Her father and mother came into the room first. After expressing their happiness, her father said, "I was thinking, *soohn*. What do you say you and I exchange houses? You need the room that we have, and we'd like a smaller place as we're getting older now. Your house will suit us better."

Ellie glanced at her husband, who looked thoughtful but not upset. "Reuben?"

He smiled at his wife, the mother of his children, before turning a grin on to his in-laws. "Sounds like a fine idea to me."

Their visitors left. Ellie gazed at her husband, overwhelmed with love for him. She saw him blink back tears as he cradled their tiny babies. "Are you *oll recht*?"

He lifted his gaze, his blue eyes shining with joy and love.

"You've given me everything, El. I love you so much."
Emotion made her voice hoarse. "I love you, husband. You've given me all I've ever wanted and more."

* * * * *

If you loved this story, check out the other books
in Rebecca Kertz's miniseries
Women of Lancaster County

A Secret Amish Love
Her Amish Christmas Sweetheart
Her Forgiving Amish Heart
Her Amish Christmas Gift

Available now from Love Inspired!

Find more great reads at www.LoveInspired.com

Dear Reader,

Welcome back to Happiness, Pennsylvania, where the Amish struggle to solve problems, marry, have children, work hard and worship God. *His Suitable Amish Wife* is Ellie Stoltzfus's story. You may have read about her four sisters, Nell, Meg, Leah and Charlie. Ellie sees her sisters happy with their husbands, and she longs for a loving husband and children of her own. But she falls for the wrong man. A widower with a little son. A man who has decided, after the death of his wife, that he won't marry for love. But he will take a wife to be the mother of his child.

Ellie shouldn't like the man, but she can see the good in him. Reuben Miller was once her sister's beau, although the couple split up after her sister realized she was in love with another man. Unwittingly, she finds herself babysitting for the man's son, and thus Ellie can't avoid Reuben. There is so much to worry about. So much to overcome. But Ellie has a strength about her that guides her with the Lord's help. Now if only the man would cooperate.

I hope you enjoy Ellie's story. She is a young woman who takes responsibility seriously, someone who needs her happily-ever-after with the man she loves.

Blessings and light,
Rebecca

SPECIAL EXCERPT FROM

*Read on for a sneak peek at
the second heartwarming book in
Lee Tobin McClain's Safe Haven series,*
Low Country Dreams!

Yasmin shifted on the glider, set it rocking with one foot and tucked the other foot up under her. The air was cooling now, a slight breeze bringing the fragrance of oleander flowers. It seemed only natural for Liam to shuffle closer on the glider. To let his arm curve around her shoulders.

Yasmin's breath whooshed out of her. Talking with Liam about her brother had made her feel vulnerable, but also relieved. Less alone. She remembered when she could share anything with Liam and he would always have her back. Such a wonderful feeling, especially after her brother had stopped being able to be that rock and that support to her.

Now Liam turned to meet her gaze head-on. His hand rose to brush back a curl that had escaped her ponytail. "I like your hairstyle," he said unexpectedly, his voice a tone deeper than usual. "Reminds me of the old days, when we were in school."

"In other words, I look like a kid?" Her words came out breathy, and she couldn't take her eyes off him.

Slowly, Liam shook his head. "Oh, no, Yasmin. You don't look like a kid at all." His eyes flickered down to her mouth, then back to her eyes.

Yasmin's heart fluttered like a terrified bird. Her stomach, her chest, all that was inside her felt squeezed by warm hands, melting.

How she wanted this. This opportunity to talk to Liam in a low, intimate voice. To feel that sense of promise, that there was something happy and bright in their future together.

O633

She tried to grasp on to the reasons why this couldn't happen. How she didn't dare to have children, because the risk of them developing a mental illness was so high. Not only because of Josiah, although that was the main thing, of course. But also because of her mother's issues.

As if all of that wasn't enough, Yasmin knew she wasn't past the safe age herself. What if she got into a relationship and then started having delusions and hearing voices?

It was hard enough taking care of her brother, her blood relative. She owed him and bore the burden gladly. But she couldn't expect a romantic partner to do the same for her, wouldn't want someone to.

Wouldn't want Liam to.

If she let things go where they were headed right now, if she let him kiss her, she wasn't sure she would have the strength to push him away again. Doing it once had nearly killed her. Maybe she could be strong enough, but only if she put an end to this before getting closer. "I think we should go."

His head tilted to one side, his eyes steady on her. "Do you really think so?"

She hesitated, clung for just a moment to the possibility of not being the responsible one, the caretaker, the one who took charge of things and tried to make everything work out. She could let herself do what she wanted to do every now and then, couldn't she? She could be spontaneous, go with her emotions, her heart.

But no. Her duty was clear. Her life was about taking care of her family, not about indulging in something pleasurable for now, but ultimately dangerous to someone she cared about. Liam was too good of a man, had suffered too many of life's blows already, to be shackled with Yasmin's issues. "Yes," she said firmly. "I really think so."

Don't miss Lee Tobin McClain's
Low Country Dreams, *available June 2019*
wherever Harlequin® books and ebooks are sold.

www.Harlequin.com